INFECTED:
THE FLIGHT

© 2015 by Caleb Cleek
All rights reserved.

Cover photos and design by Caleb Cleek.

ISBN 978-1511605458

This book is a work of fiction. All names, characters, events, and places are a product of the author's imagination or used fictitiously. Any similarity to a real person, location or business is purely coincidental.

Scripture taken from the New King James Version. Copyright 1982 by Thomas Nelson, Inc Used by permission. All rights reserved.

For
Eli, Kyle, Ellie, Abby,
and, of course, Heather

Recap of *Infected: The Fall*

A bus carrying Japanese tourists stopped in the small, remote town of Lost Hills for lunch. Connor, a local sheriff deputy, was finishing his meal when the tourists entered Mary's Diner. It quickly became apparent that the tourists were infected with an unknown sickness. Shortly after entering the diner, a woman passed out and quickly succumbed to the illness. Additional tourists soon expired from the mysterious sickness. Fearing the epidemic may spread to the rest of the town, Connor quarantined the diner and contacted Doc Baker, a local physician.

Thirty minutes after falling to the illness, the first victim revived from her apparent death in a fury, attacking Connor. Unable to match her new strength and invulnerability to pain, Connor shot her. The woman stubbornly refused to die until he placed his third shot between her eyes.

Doc Baker contacted a medical school roommate, Dr. Clark, seeking guidance with handling the disease. Dr. Clark, who worked at the CDC, revealed classified information to Doc Baker informing him that the illness was the result of a Chinese bio-weapon. Investigation revealed the Chinese had infected a private flight carrying the Japanese tourists with the weapon prior to their landing in America. The airborne infection resulted in a death-like coma, during which the body underwent massive metabolic changes. When the infected person awoke from the coma, he had superhuman strength and very aggressive, cannibalistic tendencies.

While Connor was battling the infection in Mary's Diner, a local woman, Claire Mantel, was exposed to the disease by a tourist who decided to buy souvenirs rather than eat lunch with the rest of the group. Fearing the outbreak of an epidemic, Claire and her two boys fled Lost Hills and Vista County.

Already on alert to the possibility of the Chinese releasing the bio-weapon, the government dispatched two teams of Homeland Security agents to act as an early cleanup crew. The government also sent a small Army Reserve unit to set up the first stages of quarantine for the area.

When Connor was unable to maintain his quarantine at the diner, he went home to spend his last hours with his wife Katie and son Toby, who had also been exposed. When the three failed to come down with symptoms of the disease, it was discovered that they shared a genetic immunity. Dr. Clark related that in order for a child to be immune, both parents had to have immunity. All of the offspring of two immune parents would be immune.

Realizing he was immune, Connor returned to town to assist his friend and fellow deputy, Matt. In Connor's absence, Matt discovered the Homeland Security team had been sent to kill anybody exposed to the infection in an effort to stop the spread.

Connor and Matt found out that the Homeland Security team had been dispatched to Connor's home after discovering the family had been exposed. The two deputies returned to Connor's home to confront the team which had been indiscriminately killing in town. The confrontation ended in a shootout that left all the agents dead and Katie wounded.

A retired surgeon tended to Katie's injury and sent Connor to the local pharmacy for medication. The pharmacy had been ransacked, all the narcotics stolen, and the pharmacist murdered.

Realizing that society was falling apart, the deputies moved Matt's wife, Eve, and his son, Luke, out of town to Connor and Katie's home in the country.

The next day, as they tried to maintain order in town and prepare the community for the inevitable loss of power, Connor and Matt met the Army unit that had been sent to set up the initial quarantine around town. The unit was undermanned and poorly equipped for the job they were sent to perform; however, they indicated they would do whatever they could to assist the deputies. The senior officer, Captain Tuttle, and a former Delta Force medic, Zachariah (Zack) Glenn, befriended the deputies. They also delivered a handful of vaccines for Connor to dispense to key people in the community.

As community leaders rapidly died from the infection or were killed by the infected, Connor decided to administer vaccines to Matt's wife and son, as well as to Doctor Kemp.

As the day progressed, the deputies discovered that the perpetrator of the previous night's murder and several other assaults was a local drug dealer, Curtis White. Curtis used the chaos of the spreading infection to run rampant in the community, kidnapping, robbing, and killing, and finally attacking Connor and Matt prior to escaping to a secluded, abandoned farm in the hills out of town. Realizing Curtis was going to continue killing and robbing the vulnerable survivors, the deputies decided he had to be dealt with. With the company of Zack and a local friend, Jeb Black, a former Marine and son of a local farmer, they made a night time cross country scouting trip to Curtis's hideout.

Upon their arrival, they discovered Curtis wasn't there. He had left earlier to attempt to procure the highly armed Humvees from the Army Reservists. In a sneak attack, Curtis and his followers overcame the undermanned unit and took their equipment, including the heavy guns. In the process of searching for Curtis, Jeb, who had been exposed to the infection, sacrificed himself to save Connor, Matt and Zack.

Upon returning to an area with cell phone coverage, Connor received a one word text message from Katie, "Help!"

Zack stayed at the sight of the ambush with the injured Sgt. Martinez, the sole survivor from the army unit, while Connor and Matt rushed to Connor's home, fearing the worst for their families.

Prologue

From *Infected: The Fall*

I fell to my knees and wept in front of the charred remains of my home, my head bowed forward in anguish.

When I had pulled into the driveway five minutes earlier, I was shocked by the smoking rubble that had been my house. Earlier in the afternoon, everything was fine. There had been no problems.

The sight of my smoldering home added to the steady stream of adrenaline my body had been releasing throughout the previous day and a half. I bolted from the open body Jeep, my legs wobbly from the latest adrenaline dump, and sprinted to the still smoking pile of scorched wood and heat-twisted metal, Matt on my heels. Our flashlights threw separate beams of light that ended in egg shaped spheres of illumination. The two spheres danced randomly across the charred remains of my house as we ran forward. The overwhelming stench of smoke erased every other odor. Together, we combed through the rubble and located five adult corpses.

Heat from the fire had burned the bodies beyond recognition. There was no way of telling whether they were male or female. All that remained were charred masses that roughly resembled the forms of human bodies. Three were congregated in what had been one of the bathrooms. The fourth and fifth were laying close to where the back door had been.

When Matt and I had left the house in the afternoon, five adults, including Katie and Eve, had been there. Toby and Luke were there, too. We searched frantically, looking for the boys' bodies. Protruding from the edge of a collapsed pile of rock and brick, which formed the last remembrance of the fire place, Matt located what appeared to be the barrel and action of one of the rifles the boys had been carrying when we last saw them. The fire had reduced the stock of the rifle to ashes. I reached down to pull the barrel free and burned my hands on the sweltering metal.

Looking around, I found one of Toby's shoes at the edge of the mountain of rubble. It was mostly burned. Somehow, enough remained that it was recognizable. Through bleary eyes, I started trying to move the remnants of the collapsed fireplace, searching for Toby and Luke. The intact pieces were too big to move and besides that, they were still too hot. Matt finally pulled me away, trying to console me. He had lost just as much as I had. His voice was too broken to be understood. His unintelligible consolations did little more than stoke the pain of our loss.

I slowly dragged myself from the house and headed back toward the jeep, leaving Matt alone in the grey and black nightmare. Halfway to the Jeep, I turned back and took in the sight of complete destruction.

That was when I fell to my knees and begged God to let me wake. But I didn't. You don't wake up from reality. All I could do was kneel in the dry, powdery dirt, and sob uncontrollably.

I don't know how long I knelt in front of my house. My thoughts were dominated by a single idea: there was no point in continuing. My family was gone. The world was destroyed. I had done everything in my power to alter the outcome. Nothing I had done in the last day and a half had mattered. There was nothing left to keep me here. The more I dwelt on it, the closer I came to self-destruction.

It was an end that had never seemed possible in the past. Now it was the only end that made sense. My subconscious was fighting against it, trying to convince me it wasn't the solution. My conscious mind said it was the only solution. I pulled my pistol from the holster. Holding it in my hand, I looked at the contours in the moonlight. My decision was made.

Matt's voice called in the distance and brought me back from my internal struggle, back to the world of raw and brutal pain. "Connor?" Only one word, nothing else followed. His inflection made it more of a question than a statement.

I didn't answer. I wanted to be left alone in my pain. I wanted to allow my thoughts to run to completion, to reach the point that led to the action I knew was inevitable, an end to the agony.

"Connor." This time it wasn't a question. It was a statement. I ignored him.

"Connor!" This time it was urgent, a demand for a response. "Connor! Come here!"

I forced myself to stand and edged away from the abysmal pit of despair I was wallowing through. "What?" I screamed, bitter at being forced out of my pit of self-destruction. "What is it?" I yelled again, lashing out in fury when he didn't answer.

"Hurry up. Come here."

I obeyed his request in that I started walking toward him. However, there was no hurry. Each methodical step sent a puff of dry dust into the air around my feet where it danced in the beam of my flashlight. Matt was standing next to the two bodies at the back door.

"Look at this," he said, pointing his light toward the corpses on the ground.

"I don't want to look at them," I said bitterly. "That's why I was over there," I said, pointing back to where I fallen to my knees in desperation.

"No, not the bodies, look at what's next to the bodies. Look at the guns." I hadn't seen them earlier. There were two rifles lying next to the bodies. They would have been obvious in daylight. In the darkness, the flashlights cast too many shadows. The blackened metal had blended into the dark voids when we examined the area earlier. All that was left were the receivers and barrels. Like Toby's rifle, the stocks had been reduced to ashes from the heat.

"There are two guns. So what?" I asked harshly.

"Katie had an AR-15 and a shotgun. This is some type of AK-47," Matt explained patiently.

I knelt down to examine the remnants of the rifle more closely and rubbed the distorting tears from my eyes to clear my vision. He was right. The remains of the rifles in front of me were clearly constructed from folded sheet metal. The metal was in the rectangular shape of an AK-47. This wasn't Katie's gun. I had never owned an AK-47.

As I shone the flashlight around, it picked up a shiny glint a few feet to the right of the bodies. I bent over and picked up a spent shell casing. With the exception of the radius of the case neck, which had reflected my flashlight beam, it was covered with black soot. The case was short and stubby. I turned it over and rubbed my thumb across the end to clean the soot off the marking. The end of the case was stamped 7.62x39, ammo for an AK-47. It was the same caliber and type of weapon Curtis had fired at us earlier in the day. It was the same caliber he had used to kill the baby.

I looked closer at the burned body at my feet. The heat from the fire had shrunk the ligaments in the body, which drew the arms tightly to the chest. The guns beside the bodies didn't belong in my house. If the guns belonged to the bodies beside them, the bodies didn't belong in my house, either. There were now four bodies that were unaccounted for: two adults and the two boys. A spark of hope ignited within me.

I shined my light at the head of one body, searching for a clue to its identity. I methodically examined the body as I slowly moved the halo of light from the head until I had illuminated the entire body down to both feet. The fire had consumed the clothes. Small appendages, including the fingers and toes, were missing, presumably devoured by the fire. With no indication of who the corpse had been, I moved to the second body and repeated the process.

Closer investigation of the second body fanned the spark of hope into a small flame. The examination immediately revealed a small hole in the front of the head. Rolling the body over exposed a much larger hole in the back of the head. The body didn't die in the fire. I wasn't a forensic pathologist or medical examiner, but whoever this person had been showed every indication of having died from a gunshot wound to the head. Although, I hadn't located evidence to support it, the first body had probably met the same end, a fatal gunshot wound.

I withdrew my phone from my pocket and dialed Katie's number again. With the phone to my ear, I heard the electronic ring in the earpiece. It rang again. Just before the third ring, I heard another electronic ring. This one was faint and in the distance.

Matt immediately turned his head toward the sound.

"That's Katie's phone," I whispered. We spread apart and advanced on the sound. After four rings from Katie's phone, the sound died away. I ended the call and redialed the number. Several seconds later, the ringing started again. It was coming from the base of a tree thirty feet ahead. As soon as I discerned the origin of the sound, I sprinted toward it, across the uneven dirt and weeds.

The ringing quit before I reached the tree. Light from the still illuminated screen affirmed that my ears had been leading me to the correct spot. I bent down and picked up the black plastic device. It was Katie's. The ground around the tree was bare. Shading branches above had kept any vegetation from growing in their suffocating shadows. My flashlight beam danced back and forth, searching for a clue to Katie's whereabouts. There was nothing.

The initial adrenaline rush from hearing Katie's phone died away. I began my flashlight search anew, this time systematically moving the sphere of light from right to left and then moving back to the right again, revealing unsearched areas with each sweep of the beam. Three feet to the right of the trunk, the light was reflected by several shiny objects scattered over a foot or two. They were shell casings. I picked one up. The reflected light was too bright, and the glare obscured the details. I held down the power button on the back of my flashlight. A couple seconds later, the beam intensity was cut in half. A second later, the intensity of the already dimmed beam was cut in half again. At a quarter of its original brightness, the light exposed the head stamp. Winchester was emblazed around the top edge of the end of the case. .223 Rem was stamped below it. It was the brand I used for my reloads. It was the brand that was loaded in Katie's rifle when I left the house.

Returning my flashlight to full intensity, I continued my search beneath the tree. I found a second group containing three shell casings. These casings were much smaller. They were .22 long rifle cases. I picked one up. It had a C stamped where the primer would have been on a center fire case. It was the same mark that was on the CCI Mini Mags Toby shot.

My new-found hope was no longer a small flame that needed to be kindled. It suddenly erupted into a blaze that renewed my will to live.

Part 1

Lost Hills, California

Thursday Night

Chapter 1

Matt and Connor continued a systematic search around the tree, looking for some clue to the whereabouts of their families. Minutes before, they had assumed their wives and boys had died in the fire that had reduced Connor's home to a smoldering pile of rubble. Then they found evidence showing, almost without a doubt, that they had not been in the inferno as it raged out of control.

Connor turned toward Matt, his flashlight illuminating white streaks of skin from the corners of Matt's eyes, running down his soot covered face. Connor knew his face bore the same signs of anguish, anguish that had nearly pushed him past the brink of what he could handle.

Finally Connor spoke. "They aren't here anymore. Katie's car is still over there and so is your truck. They didn't drive away. They either left on foot or they were taken."

"Okay," Matt answered, his voice still broken. "Let's assume they left on foot. Where would they have gone?"

"There are two bodies in the house that don't belong there," Connor said, referring to the two charred corpses they had found in the remains of his house minutes before. One of them had what looked like a bullet hole in his head. Both had the burned remains of AK-47 rifles next to their bodies.

"Assuming the bodies belong to Curtis's crew, there must have been others. There is no way the two of them walked here. There aren't any other vehicles, so somebody drove away after the fire. Katie and Eve wouldn't have left toward the road with whoever started the fire having gone in that direction. The only place they could have gone is there," Connor said, pointing to the rugged hills rising up behind his property. "That's assuming Curtis didn't take them with him."

"No way," Matt interjected. "Based on the shell casings we found, we know Katie, Eve and the boys had at least two guns. There weren't enough casings for them to have run out of ammo. With two guns, they would have been able to put up a good fight. They wouldn't have given up with ammo to burn. Curtis didn't take them. They're out there," he said, looking at the rugged terrain behind them. "Where out there would they go, though?" he asked rhetorically. "There's a lot of country."

No sooner had the words left Matt's mouth than a soft *ffftt* whispered passed their heads and a branch on the tree behind them snapped, wood fragments flying in all directions. A fraction of a second later, the crack of a gunshot raced across Connor's property and into the distance along the hills behind the house, echoing along the rim rock like a peel of thunder.

In the second it took for them to process the sound and formulate the appropriate response, another gunshot blasted from behind the shed. This time, Connor's eyes, having been drawn to the sound of the previous shot, spotted a short burst of flame erupt as the last remnants of combusting gun powder spewed out the gun barrel and into the night. A second flame lit up the area a mere five feet from the first. There were at least two shooters.

Matt responded faster than Connor. Connor's initial response was to move for the cover of the tree behind them. Matt's first response was to rip his pistol from its holster and put lead downrange. He moved for cover as his gun spat its own short flames toward the ambushers.

Connor and Matt hunkered behind the same tree their families had used for cover a short time before. An occasional thud reverberated through the tree as it absorbed the energy of a bullet that had buried itself deep in the trunk.

The initial flurry of gunfire died to sporadic pops as both sides settled down and began looking for the outline of a target illuminated by the moon overhead.

"I'm getting sick and tired of people shooting at me," Matt hissed from two feet away in a moment of stillness. "Why is my rifle in the car every time I need it? It would come in pretty handy right now."

Connor agreed. The two shooters were at least a hundred yards away. Under the best of circumstances, it was a really long shot for a pistol. In the poorly illuminated night, it was virtually impossible to hit somebody at that distance.

"We're going to have to get closer to win this," Connor said softly. "Do you want to stay here and lay down cover fire or do you want to try to get behind them?"

"You're always telling me how fast you are. Why don't you put some of that greased lightning speed to use?" Matt quietly uttered. "I like it right here behind this tree."

"Okay," Connor said, pulling two spare magazines out of his pocket. "Take these. You won't be able to cover me very well if you run out of bullets. I'm going to crawl back a ways and try to slip out of here unnoticed," he whispered. Matt gave a nearly imperceptible nod as he slid to the right, peered around the tree, and fired into the darkness to the right of the shed. The two gunmen immediately lit up the area in front of them with several brief muzzle flashes. Bullets hit close to Matt, peppering his face with wood chips from the tree and dirt and gravel from the ground. He quickly squirmed back behind cover.

"I'm going to try to work my way up the hill to get behind them. Remember where I am when you fire," Connor admonished as he slid backwards and turned around, trying to burrow into the dirt as he scurried away on his belly.

Twenty yards from the tree, Connor started down a slight hill. When he had moved down the hill far enough to be out of sight, he transitioned to his hands and knees, quadrupling his speed. A short distance later, the crest of the hill provided enough cover that he rose to his feet, hunkered over as far as he could, and began to run.

As Connor moved away from the house, the undergrowth increased, providing additional concealment as he began a wide circle that would take him up the hill and bring him back down and behind whoever was shooting at Matt. He just hoped that the two shooters hadn't seen him leave and would stay where they were until he could get into position behind them.

His heart was racing, both from adrenaline and exertion. He consciously forced himself to slow his pace, hoping to quiet his approach as well as decrease his galloping heart rate enough to let him hit his target when he got into position.

Connor's estimation of time was distorted by the stress his body was being subjected to. He looked briefly at his watch which glowed green when he squeezed the top right button. The reading meant nothing because he had failed to look at it when he started. He estimated he had been moving for a minute or two, but it could have been more. He didn't know for sure. Matt kept up his cover fire, sending a round out every five or six seconds. With the ammo load Connor knew Matt had, he figured Matt could keep that rate of fire up for five or six minutes before he ran out of bullets. The deeper booming of the two rifles assured him that Matt had been unsuccessful in his attempts to hit either shooter.

The rifle shots came closer together than Matt's shots, and the constant booms helped Connor track his progress. By the time he estimated he was directly above the shooters, Connor had gained about eighty feet of elevation and was probably two hundred yards away from them. His circular path started him back downhill as he began flanking the attacking party. He had to continually force himself to slow, conscious of the sound he knew he was making. The constant ring in his ears overshadowed most of the noise he made and he was sure the shooters suffered from the same problem. Connor still worked to move as silently as possible.

The brush thinned and then disappeared and the shed came into view. Matt's ricochets zinged away into the night, motivating Connor to keep low. He approached the shed from forty-five degrees to the left, hoping it would keep him out of Matt's field of fire. At fifty or sixty yards, Connor saw the prone form of the first gunman come into view in the dim moonlit night. He was oblivious to

Connor's approach. As he slowly inched closer, Connor realized the second shooter had moved. Connor was now close enough to see the entire area, and there was only one person there. The second must have left to flank Matt's position. It was possible Connor had passed him in the brush and had not even realized it. Connor raised his pistol to fire and then hesitated. If the other shooter was still close by, Connor would give away his position and draw his fire.

Not knowing where the second shooter was, Connor paused, deciding how to best approach the situation. He realized that Matt hadn't fired for quite a while. The shooter in front of Connor noticed, too, and raised himself up higher. At first Connor feared Matt may have been hit, but then Matt yelled a string of insults at the shooter, daring him to show himself. It dawned on Connor that Matt was out of bullets. The shooter came to the same conclusion and rose up further, taking a solid rest on a boulder. Realizing the gunman had no clue Connor was there, Connor placed his pistol back in the holster. He pulled his knife out of his pocket and slowly opened the four-inch blade.

Hoping he was right in his assessment that Matt's ammo supply was depleted, Connor moved directly behind the shooter and into Matt's line of fire. Connor closed to three feet behind the man before he sensed Connor's presence. The shooter began to turn his head to the left. Connor lunged to his right side, grasping the gunman's chin in his left hand and pulling it all the way around to his left shoulder. He plunged the point of the knife into the now exposed right side of the shooter's neck and made two quick sawing motions. Hot sticky fluid gushed from the wound. The blade momentarily slowed as it passed through the tough cartilage of his windpipe and then freely cut again until it grated to a stop against his spine. His last breaths gurgled from his severed throat and then his body went limp, his chin slipping from Connor's grasp.

Connor briefly froze, looking in horror at the savagery he had wrought. Deserved or not, such a barbaric attack bucked and kicked at his conscience. He pushed the guilt from his mind and reached for the ambusher's rifle. As Connor lifted the AR style rifle, he saw several magazines on the ground. He picked one up and, realizing it was empty, dropped it back to the bare dirt.

Pulling the charging handle back halfway opened the action of the rifle enough for him to place a finger in and feel that there was at least one round left in the gun. Unsure of where the second shooter had gone, Connor was hesitant to remain where he was. He vainly searched the dim moonlit terrain, looking for the other assailant. The only place that made sense for him to go was up the hill following the reciprocal path that Connor had taken. How they had missed each other was a mystery. Had their ears not been ringing from the gunfire, they surely would have heard each other clumping through the undergrowth.

Connor debated yelling to alert Matt. Just before he did, he detected movement in the grassy clearing uphill from Matt's position. It was the second shooter. Had his arc had a slightly larger radius, he would have come out behind the hill Connor had used for cover as he left Matt. However, the intruder was not familiar with the terrain, and his focus on Matt had prevented him from realizing there was better cover available. Connor rolled the first shooter away from the rock and took a position behind it, feeling the sticky moistness of blood soak into his pants as he sat down. Ignoring the sensation, he rested the foreend of the rifle on the rock and looked through the sight, but couldn't see anything. Connor reached up with his left thumb and pushed on the rear site. Ninety degrees of rotation brought the larger aperture site up, which gave him the extra visibility he needed to make out the second assailant in the dim moonlight. The shooter had spotted Matt and was taking aim at him. Connor breathed in, let half the breath out, and held the rest as he applied increasing force to the trigger. It suddenly snapped, releasing a bellow from the rifle which recoiled slightly, causing him to lose sight of the target. Connor searched where he had been and saw no sign of him.

"Second shooter to your right," Connor yelled at Matt. He saw Matt's body quickly move around the tree, putting it between himself and where Connor told him the gunman was located.

"How far?" he yelled back.

"Seventy yards, maybe eighty."

"Shoot him!" he yelled.

Connor continued searching the opening. There was nothing. The guy couldn't have cleared the opening that fast. The only possibilities were that Connor had hit him and he had fallen or he had missed and the guy had dropped to his belly. Either way, he was obscured by the short grass carpeting the area. Not knowing what to do, Connor fired a round in the vicinity of where he had last seen the guy. He moved his aim slightly and fired again. Connor continued moving his aim in a grid pattern until the magazine was empty.

Then he waited.

And waited.

After two minutes had passed on his watch, Connor charged, pistol in hand, to the shooter's last known position.

He nearly stepped on the body before he saw it. Stopping just short, Connor pointed his gun at the prostrate form at his feet. He pulled the flash light from his belt and shined it on the body. It was a male in his late twenties, and he was still alive, his chest soaked in blood. The bright red, frothy fluid around his mouth suggested he was shot through the lung.

"Help me," he wheezed.

"Not until you help me," Connor seethed back at him. "Where are my wife and son?"

The man tried to answer, but the words wouldn't come. He silently mouthed something Connor couldn't make out. He coughed, spraying a mist of blood out into the night. His arm feebly rose to wipe his mouth, smearing the blood across his face.

Connor pulled his knife back out of his pocket, the handle still slick with blood. He dropped the naked blade to the guy's chest and sliced the blood-soaked fabric of his shirt open from top to bottom, revealing a quarter inch hole through the well-formed muscle on the right side of his chest. Blood bubbled from the hole, which emitted a sucking sound with every breath he took.

"Matt, I need your help," Connor yelled. Instantly, he heard Matt thudding toward him through the dry grass and sticks. Ten seconds later, Matt was by his side. "He's hit in the chest," Connor advised without emotion. "He can't breathe. Help me roll him on his side."

They moved the man onto his left side revealing another

hole in his back, this one much larger than the first. "See if you can seal that hole up," Connor said, handing him a rubber glove from his pocket.

Matt firmly pressed the glove against the man's back, covering the hole and sealing it from the outside. Connor rolled the man onto his back again with Matt's arm beneath, holding the glove in place. Connor took the other glove and placed it over the entrance hole when the man's chest contracted, hoping to seal it and allow his good lung to fill with air through his mouth rather than his chest cavity filling with air through the holes in it. The next time his diaphragm expanded, the look of relief on his face assured them he was getting at least a little air into his lung.

"Now answer my question or I'm going to move my hand and let you suffocate. Where are our families?"

"Curtis took them to the ranch," he gasped.

Chapter 2

True to their word, after he provided the information they sought, Matt and Connor tended to his injury as best they could. Within minutes he succumbed to the wound and drifted from this life to the next. Neither Matt nor Connor mourned his passing.

"We have to get them back before Curtis does something that can't be undone," Matt snarled bitterly as he turned back to the tree he had used for cover. Connor silently followed him, trying to formulate a plan as they walked.

They quickly collected the pistol magazines Matt had dropped around the tree as the bullets ran out.

"Are there any forty cal bullets in the shed or did they all get put in the house?" Matt questioned.

The day before, they had moved a large quantity of bullets from the sheriff's station to Connor's house. Most of the bullets had been secured inside the house, but they had placed a couple dozen cases in his tool shed. All of the bullets they stored in the house were destroyed in the fire, leaving only what was left in the shed.

"Most of the forties were burned, but I think there are a couple cases in the shed," Connor answered.

Connor picked up the empty AR magazines outside the shed while Matt retrieved a case of .40 bullets. With their hands full, they quickly returned to the Jeep they had left parked in front of Connor's smoldering home.

"I'm keeping this thing on me from here on out," Matt said as he placed his rifle sling over his shoulder, leaving the gun hanging from his chest. "I won't be caught without it again. Let's pick up Zack and Martinez and go get Curtis." Matt's face had hardened to an unreadable slate, giving no indication of the emotions raging through his mind. Even so, Connor understood what Matt was feeling because he was feeling the same things.

The rage that had been building within Connor over the past two days was about to boil beyond his ability to contain. The dam would break, and whoever was in his path would be annihilated. Beside the rage was a welling sense of panic. Curtis had kidnapped his family, and he was terrified by what Curtis would do to them. He had proven himself to be a homicidal sociopath. The only reason he would keep them alive was that he thought he could gain something by doing so. The fact that he had taken them and not killed them on the spot produced a small ray of hope, but he could change his mind at any moment.

It didn't take long to return to where they had left Zachariah Glenn and Sgt. Martinez, the two surviving members of the Army reserve unit that had been sent to Lost Hills to establish a perimeter around town in hopes of stopping the spread of the infection. Earlier in the night, Curtis had ambushed the three teams and taken their Humvees and heavy weapons. Martinez, the sole survivor of the attacks, had been wounded and left for dead. Zack had been with Matt and Connor during the attack. After finding Martinez wounded, Zack stayed to care for him when Connor had received a text from his wife, Katie, with a frantic cry for help.

Zack and Sgt. Martinez had moved to the edge of the field where Martinez had been found. The four dead soldiers from Martinez's team had been laid side by side in front of the dilapidated old barb wire fence that separated the shin-high alfalfa from the roadway.

"Martinez has a bad concussion, but he's going to be okay," Zack announced. "That said, he's a lucky man; look at this." He shined his flashlight on the left side of Martinez's skull, which was covered in a blood-soaked bandage that encircled his head. "A bullet hit him right there," he said, pointing above his ear, "and split his scalp all the way down the side. Half an inch to the right and it would have been lights out for sure. Where did you guys run off to?" he asked, realizing something was bothering them besides the slaughter of his teammates.

"Curtis hit my house while we were doing recon on his place. He burned it to the ground and took our families." As Connor said it, the lump began building in his throat again. He didn't trust himself to say more.

Zack took a step toward him and put a hand on Connor's shoulder. "We're going to get them back. Where can we leave Martinez?"

Matt pulled his phone from his pocket, dialed a number, and placed it to his ear. A moment later he started talking. As he talked, he moved away from Zack and Connor. He hung up the phone, walked back, and said, "Frank said we can leave Martinez at his parents' place. He's going to come with us. There's no talking him out of it."

"Does he know about Jeb?" Connor asked.

"I didn't tell him the specifics. All I said was that one of

THE FLIGHT

Curtis's guys shot him before the infection took him."

Except for the squeaky suspension of the Jeep, the ride to the Black's farm was silent. Nobody said a word. Martinez moaned occasionally when the shocks failed to fully absorb a bump in the road.

The Blacks' home had been transformed from the welcoming residence Connor had last visited to a boarded up garrison. Pine two by fours, separated by eight inch gaps, overlaid all of the ground floor windows, their unpainted surfaces marring the appearance of an otherwise immaculately maintained farmhouse. The second story windows were unobstructed, but were shut tight. Normally on a summer night, country windows were left open to permit the cooling breeze to blow away the stifling afternoon air. Tonight, no chances were being taken.

Before they could exit the Jeep, Frank bounded down the stairs from the porch, followed by his dad. They met Connor as he slid across the torn fabric that covered the driver's seat of the Jeep. The duo drew up three feet short and Frank's dad, Merv, extended his hand.

"I'm sorry about Jeb," Connor said as he shook Merv's hand. "He died saving our lives tonight."

Merv nodded his head, eyes blinking. His voice broke as he said, "He would have…" he paused trying to compose himself. "That sounds like Jeb."

Frank moved to the passenger side to assist Zack as he eased Martinez out of the vehicle. They helped him inside as Matt and Connor filled Merv in on the details of what had happened to Jeb.

Tears flowed down the old rancher's leathery cheeks as the story unfolded and he heard of his son's exposure to the infection and of his selfless death.

Frank and Zack bounded down the steps toward Connor and Matt

After the events regarding Jeb were related, Connor turned to Matt. "I'm going to stop by the station and pick up some more rifle mags and ammunition. When Frank has his gear together, have him drive you guys over there. I'll have everything ready when you arrive, and we won't have to waste any more time."

As Connor fired up the Jeep's engine, Merv said, "Take care, Connor," and turned back to the house.

Chapter 3

Looting had started in town. Store windows were broken out with dropped goods trailing to the parking lot. Connor passed several infected walking aimlessly in the streets. They turned as he passed, but showed no real interest in him. Perhaps, in the darkness, all they could see and hear was the squeaky Jeep. Perhaps they didn't realize there was a meal in the driver seat. Whatever the reason, they ignored him and he didn't have time to do anything about them.

Connor parked in back of the station behind a locked gate and fence topped with concertina wire. He hurried inside to collect the ammo and extra magazines they would need for the raid to free Katie, Eve, and the boys.

As he thumbed round after round of nickel plated cartridges into magazines, Connor heard the motor of a vehicle as it pulled up to the sidewalk in front of the station. He increased his pace, frustrated that he hadn't finished before they arrived.

As he continued to hurriedly shove bullets into hungry magazines, he heard glass shatter in the lobby. Connor quickly dropped the magazine he was loading, picked up one of the rifles, and racked a round into the chamber. A moment later, he heard a foul string of obscenities followed by, "Dude, you cut yourself bad."

"You think I don't know that?" the voice belonging to

the obscenities growled angrily.

"You're dripping blood all over the floor. They can test that for DNA. They keep a sample of your DNA in a data base when you go to prison. All they have to do is put your blood in the machine and they will know you were here," the voice said in distress.

"Are you stupid? They don't keep your DNA and even if they did, there's nobody left to care," the obscene voice said irritably as it kept pace with the boot falls clicking their way down the hallway.

"Both of you shut up. Let's get the guns and ammo and get back to the ranch before Paul gets into trouble. Not only is he incompetent, but I don't trust him to keep his hands off the women even though I told him they're mine," a third voice interrupted angrily. "I don't want those women spoiled before I get to enjoy them myself."

Connor had been moving toward the open doorway when the third person spoke. His body stiffened and his heart rate spiked at the sound of Curtis's voice. Connor raised his rifle to his shoulder and flicked the safety selector to fire as he spun around the doorway and into the hall, locking eyes with Curtis, who was a step behind the two men who had been arguing. Both of them had guns in their hands. Before they had time to register the threat Connor presented, he had already pulled the trigger twice, smashing two slugs through the chest of the thug on the right. Before his crumpling body had fallen to the ground, Connor had already jerked his rifle to the left. A rapid double tap to the center of his forehead sent the second member of the trio falling in a heap to the floor.

Satisfaction flooded through Connor's body as he aligned his sites on the center of Curtis's startled face and pulled the trigger.

Chapter 4

Nothing happened.

He pulled the trigger again, this time jerking it backwards in desperation.

Nothing.

A smirk appeared on Curtis's face as they simultaneously realized the rifle had jammed. He lunged at Connor from six feet away.

Connor thrust the barrel of the rifle toward the bridge of Curtis's nose. Seeing the impending blow, Curtis tilted his head to the right and took a glancing impact to his left cheek. As he slipped passed the end of the rifle, Curtis's left hand grasped the weapon's forend and pushed it to the side as his right fist began an arcing haymaker toward the side of Connor's head.

Knowing he could not dodge the punch, Connor lunged into it while it was still in its inception and before it had built the momentum necessary to do any damage to him. The blow caught the left side of Connor's head without any real force.

Connor parried with a left hook that landed solidly below Curtis's right eye, but they were in such close proximity that Connor's punch had little effect. It momentarily distracted Curtis without causing any significant damage.

Curtis unleashed a flurry of punches at Connor's head, but Connor was able to deflect most of them with his raised left arm. Curtis moved in close and wrapped his right hand around the back of Connor's head and drew it toward himself. Curtis released his grip on the rifle and clawed at Connor's eyes.

Since Connor couldn't shoot the jammed rifle and they were too close to use it as a club, he threw it behind him to keep it out of Curtis's hands. Connor ducked his head protectively as he tried to pull away from Curtis's grasp. His hand dropped for his pistol to end the fight, but Curtis sensed the movement and gripped the top of the slide as Connor pulled it free of the holster. Connor pulled the trigger as the muzzle cleared leather, but Curtis had redirected the barrel clear of his torso and the bullet buried itself in the wall at the end of the hallway. Connor pulled the gun backwards and the barrel came back in line with Curtis. He pulled the trigger again and nothing happened. Curtis's grip on the slide had kept the action from cycling and drawing a fresh bullet from the magazine. Connor was left with nothing but a club over which they continued to struggle.

As Connor fought to maintain his grip on the pistol, Curtis pummeled him again and again with crushing right handed blows to his face. With each blow, Connor's vision momentarily darkened. He wrenched his right hand away from Curtis, the pistol slipping from his hand, but in the process, Connor lost his grip as well and the two and a half pounds of plastic, ceramic, and steel clattered across the floor behind them. With his right hand free, Connor swung savagely with an uppercut to Curtis's jaw and sent him staggering backwards.

Curtis lowered his head and charged Connor in an attempt to take the fight to the ground. Knowing Curtis frequented the local MMA gym, Connor wasn't going to let him take the fight into his comfort zone.

Connor sidestepped and smashed his fist down into the back of Curtis's head in a hammer blow. Already off balance, Curtis crashed onto his stomach. Connor lashed out with his foot, kicking Curtis in the side.

Connor knew better than to think this was a gentleman's fight with rules. It was a no-holds-barred brawl to the death. At best, only one of them would survive.

Curtis grunted as Connor's boot drove the air from his lungs. Before Connor regained his balance, Curtis's right leg snaked out in a blurred, arching motion and swept Connor's feet off the ground. With his base knocked from beneath him, Connor toppled to his back. Curtis scampered across the floor and lay across Connor's chest as he swung his leg over Connor's stomach and achieved a full mount, sitting astride Connor's abdomen with a leg on either side. Connor bent his arms ninety degrees at the elbows and brought them up over his face to deflect the death that was raining down from above in the form of one monstrous blow after another. His mouth was full of blood, his ears rang, and his vision was going in and out.

Connor knew he wouldn't survive long in this position. With all the strength he could muster, he pushed with his legs and bucked his hips up as far as he could. Curtis lost his balance and fell forward, his hands falling to the ground as he came to rest on all fours, his hands and knees straddling Connor.

Connor wrapped the crook of his elbow around Curtis's

right arm and pulled it inward as he bucked his hips again. With the support of his right arm pulled away, Curtis's body tumbled to the right as Connor knocked him off balance. As Curtis fell, Connor rolled into him, his momentum driving Curtis off and onto the floor.

Having quickly realized he was no match for Curtis in a grappling fight, Connor used the momentary reprieve to regain his footing rather than attempt to gain the advantage on the ground. He staggered backwards, trying to create distance between them to give his senses time to return before he pressed the attack.

Realizing he was losing his advantage on the ground, Curtis lunged at Connor's ankles, trying to trip him up and drive him back to the floor. Connor lashed out with his foot and kicked Curtis in the face. His boot thudded solidly, rocking his enemy's head backwards.

Connor's brain had been beaten into a thick fog. He reached for his pistol and his hand grasped desperately into the empty holster until he realized the gun wasn't there. Confused, he reached to the opposite side of his belt for his Taser, but in his state of delirium, he couldn't remember how to work the release to free it from the holster. In the struggle on the ground, Connor's baton had worked its way out of the ring on his belt. He had no advantage to use over Curtis as he rose to his feet. Curtis looked at him, realized the bad state Connor was in, and smiled. Two dark voids filled the place where his top teeth had been moments before. Connor's desperate kick had driven them from his gums.

Curtis turned his head to the side and spit. A red glob of blood and saliva struck the wall and slowly rolled downwards, leaving a trail behind like a slug inching its way toward the floor.

Connor lethargically shook his head in a futile attempt to free the cobwebs that were inhibiting his ability to think and move. Curtis, sensing victory, smiled wider. "Don't worry, Buddy," he said arrogantly with blood dripping from the corner of his mouth. "I'll end this quick and put you out of your misery." He wiped his forearm across his lips, pulling most of the blood away but smearing a streak across his cheek. "Then I'm going back up to my place in the hills to get acquainted with your family. I'm going to start by slitting your little brat's throat in front of Mommy to erase any doubts from her mind about who's in charge. Then I'm going spend some quality time alone with her, if you know what I mean." His braying laughter filled the narrow hallway as he advanced toward Connor.

Connor's eyes were unable to focus. The repeated blows to his head left him seeing twin images of Curtis standing in front of him.

Fury overwhelmed Connor; fury at the fact that Curtis had ruined so many lives over the last twenty four hours, fury at the people Connor knew who had been killed by the infection and the infected, fury at the government for attacking their community, but mostly, it was fury at himself. He realized he was going to lose this fight and leave Katie and Toby with nobody to stand between them and this vile, wretched man. Matt, Frank and Zack would continue on without him, but they would arrive too late. Curtis would have already committed his barbaric acts of violence against Connor's family.

"I'm going to enjoy killing you almost as much as I'm going to enjoy acquainting myself with your wife," Curtis taunted. "And there is nothing you can do to stop me."

Connor back peddled, trying to give his head time to clear. He took another step and then another. Curtis kept coming, matching Connor's speed step for step, no longer feeling the urgency of pressing the attack. Curtis was enjoying his victory lap, basking in what he perceived to be imminent triumph. As Connor continued backwards, clarity began returning to his thoughts and the two images before him joined together as his brain regained the fine control over the lenses in his eyes and they once again focused in conjunction on a single point in space.

Connor's head still throbbed. Rivulets of blood continued trickling into his left eye from a gash in his forehead. What had to be a broken rib rattled with every breath, but Connor's determination to kill Curtis solidified. Hatred toward Curtis and what he stood for grew along with the rage that had been building since the outbreak in the diner. Connor clenched his fists and raised them to defend himself as he took a step forward toward the death that awaited one of them.

Curtis led with an arcing right. Connor ducked beneath and answered with a hard left jab to Curtis's unprotected nose. His head rolled back, pivoting at the neck and Connor followed with a right jab and a left hook, both of which rocked Curtis to his heels.

Curtis staggered back two steps before he regained his balance. Connor pressed forward, swinging wildly with both fists, leaving his face unguarded. Seeing the opening, Curtis sidestepped a punch and answered with a hard jab that opened the flood gates behind Connor's nose. Blood burst forth and his eyes were flooded with tears. Connor coughed as the blood running down the back of his throat momentarily threatened to choke him.

They stood toe to toe, swapping devastating blows at an unsustainable rate. Connor's lungs gasped for air as his muscles greedily extracted every molecule of oxygen available to them. His muscles burned from fatigue and yet he continued to swing, matching Curtis blow for blow.

Curtis shot in close, once again wrapping his arm around the back of Connor's head, holding it in place while he pummeled it with his free hand. Connor brought his knee up solidly into Curtis's groin, crushing everything between his knee and Curtis's pelvis. Curtis howled in agony but refused to release his clench on Connor's head. Connor landed a solid blow into Curtis's abdomen, loosening his grip enough for Connor to raise his head fully erect. Tucking his hand in close to his body, Connor's elbow whipped through the air and smashed into Curtis's temple, splitting the skin and loosing a river of blood which cascaded down the side of his face. Curtis reeled backwards and would have fallen to the floor had the wall not been behind him. Connor willed his body forward to continue the attack, but it momentarily refused to obey, having been racked with exhaustion.

They eyed each other, five feet apart, searching for a weakness to exploit. Curtis's hand slinked into his pocket and withdrew a knife. With the press of a button, a stainless steel blade streaked up, locking in place with a snap. Holding the knife in close to his side, blade facing up, he stepped toward Connor.

Connor's eyes focused on the razor edge as it darted at him without warning. He slapped it aside, inches short of it burrowing its way into the tender flesh of his stomach. Curtis's torn lips parted in a bloody grin as the knife arced toward Connor's ribs. The blade cut deeply into his side before grating against the bone. Connor reached for Curtis's hand, but he had already withdrawn it. If not for the sticky wetness running down his side, Connor would not have known he had been cut. There was no sensation of pain.

Connor fumbled for his Taser again, but Curtis's attack was unrelenting. He didn't leave a chance for Connor to drop his left hand from its defensive position long enough to draw the electronic weapon. Curtis lunged again and Connor twisted to the side, this time catching Curtis's wrist in his hand. He struggled to maintain his hold while he battered Curtis's head with his free fist. Pushing the knife to the side, Connor dropped his shoulder and plowed into Curtis, driving him into the wall behind. The wall's impact to his kidneys took Curtis's breath away and left him momentarily stunned. Connor gripped the bottom of the knife handle that was extending below Curtis's hand and twisted it up and between his fingers, freeing it from Curtis's steely hold.

With the knife now in his uncontested control, Connor struck out and the blade sank, unfettered, into Curtis's unprotected chest. Curtis gasped as Connor withdrew the blade and sank it in again and again, releasing a torrent of blood which rapidly soaked through the fabric of Curtis's white t-shirt.

Realizing he had been dealt a fatal blow, Curtis ceased his struggle. He slowly slid down the wall coming to rest on his knees, his hands gripping the handle of the knife extending out of his chest. Lacking the strength to withdraw the protruding instrument of death, he slowly panted, his eyes locked onto Connor's.

"Do you know what I'm going to miss the most?" Curtis

asked, wheezing as he spoke. "I'm going to miss the opportunity to get to know your wife." Curtis broke into a grin and coughed, spewing blood on Connor.

In his peripheral vision, Connor saw his pistol on the ground at his feet. He bent to pick it up and stumbled to his knees. The gun still lay at his side. Willing his hand to do his bidding in spite of exhaustion, Connor picked the pistol up. Racking the slide, he freed the empty casing that was blocking the action. He aligned the sites with Curtis's smiling face and pulled the trigger, sending him on a one way journey into the fiery blazes of the hottest furnaces of Hades.

The pistol slipped from Connor's hands and clattered to the ground. He leaned back against the wall and stared in complete exhaustion at his defeated nemesis.

Chapter 5

Connor must have passed out because he had no recollection of anything until he heard voices and felt hands shaking him. He opened his eyes to see Matt hovering over him. From the looks he was getting from Matt, Frank and Zack, Connor realized the beating he received must have left him looking pretty pathetic.

Zack, pushing Matt aside, began examining Connor. "What hurts?" he asked as he unbuttoned Connor's blood-soaked shirt.

"Mmm," Connor moaned. The brain fog had returned with a vengeance. "A better question is what doesn't hurt," he muttered past his split and swollen lips, trying without success to focus on the individual aches and pains. All he was getting from his brain was pain, pain everywhere. He couldn't isolate any individual sensations.

Zack poked and prodded without speaking. He started with Connor's head, shining a light in his eyes after prying open the swollen upper and lower eyelids on his left eye. He felt Connor's neck and then felt his way down his torso, feeling from side to side across his ribs. "Nice cut you got there." Zack said, as he ran a finger along its length. "I assume you're not going to want any anesthetic before I sew it up?"

"I'm not falling for that one again," Connor stammered nearly incoherently.

"I hope you got those magazines all loaded up before you got beat to a pulp," Zack said, pushing on Connor's stomach with both hands. "We passed a whole passel of infected on the way over here," he continued.

"We don't have time for this," Connor said, trying to push Zack away. "Curtis's guys have Katie, Eve, and the boys. Even Curtis was worried about what was going to happen before he caught up with them." As Connor paused to cough, pain shot through his chest. His head felt like it would burst. "We have to go. Now!" he said, trying to impress the urgency he felt on the others.

"We're secure here," Zack said, turning to Frank. "Go out to the truck and bring the package inside."

Frank, who had been kneeling beside Connor, stood up and walked nonchalantly down the hall.

Anger welled up within Connor. Nobody had the sense of urgency the situation demanded. Everybody was calm and relaxed. Zack had an infuriating smirk on his face when he turned back to Connor and continued his examination. He worked his way down Connor's legs, pushing and pulling as he went.

"Matt, tell him we don't have time for this!" Connor asserted as he pushed himself upright, growing more agitated at the lack of urgency everybody was exhibiting.

Zack put his hand on Connor's chest, bringing a halt to his rising. He put his other hand behind Connor's head and pushed him back to the floor. "You need to take it easy, Buddy," he said calmly but insistently. "You have a nasty concussion, at least one broken rib and your guts are probably beat to a jelly inside of you. You are in no condition to..." and he was cut short.

"Get out of my way!" Connor heard as Katie came into his field of vision and pushed Zack to the side. Her mouth opened and her lips quivered as she looked at him. Her cobalt eyes began to sparkle as the tears built up and overflowed down her cheeks.

Zack removed his pack and began pulling things out of different pockets as Katie bent down, hugging Connor and kissing his broken and bloody lips. When she pulled back, her green shirt had dark splotches of blood all over and her lips were smeared with blood, too.

"Oh, Connor, are you okay?" she sobbed.

"I don't understand," Connor said with confusion, seeing Toby, Eve and Luke behind Katie, all with equally distraught looks on their faces.

"Mom, is he going to die?" Toby asked, nearing the point of tears.

"No sweetie, he's not going to die," Katie said, looking to Zack for reassurance.

"Your mom's right. He's not going to die. He's going to be pretty sore for a while, but he's going to be fine." Zack affirmed. After cleaning the wound, Zack interrupted the reunion between the family. "Hang on, Connor. You're going to feel some pricks," he added as he bent over with a syringe in his hand.

Connor watched as he injected a clear liquid along the length of the gash on his side. He didn't feel a thing after the initial pokes. After recapping the syringe, Zack prepared the curved needle and thread he pulled from a packet in his bag. He plunged the needle in one side of the cut and out the other, continuing along the whole length with a running stitch. Blood oozed out as he pulled the stitch tight and brought the two sides of the cut together. In a well-practiced motion, he knotted the suture, trimmed the ends, and threw both hands above his head, yelling, "Done!"

With everybody staring at him in confusion, Zack explained, "Haven't you guys ever been to a rodeo? I used to do high school rodeo calf roping."

A half smile brightened Katie's face and Matt shook his head back and forth and whispered, "He's a strange dude," to Toby and Luke. They both nodded in agreement, grins plastered on their faces, as they looked at Zack in awe.

Chapter 6

The mood in the hallway was suddenly much lighter. There was talking and even some laughter. Connor had a hard time taking it in at first, but as his brain began to clear, his thoughts came easier and more cohesively. Eventually, he was able to put together the nagging question that had been lurking in the back of his mind. As soon as he was able to put it into words, Connor asked, "How did you get away from Curtis?"

Eve started for the group, "It was really Luke and Toby who did it."

"Yeah," Luke said. "They caught us at your house and tied us up and put us in the back of the Army truck. That guy right there," he pointed at Curtis's body, "told them to take us to the ranch. He and the guys in his Army truck and the other one went somewhere together and two guys in our truck went the other way. When we passed the grocery store, one of the guys said they should stop and get some booze. When they stopped, they left us in the truck. I got my hand untied and then I untied Toby. They had put handcuffs on Mom and Katie and we couldn't get them off."

"One of the guys left his rifle in the truck," Toby added. "I got it out of the front seat. It was just like yours, Dad," he added, the excitement building in his voice. "At first I couldn't turn the safety off, but then I remembered it was on the side of the gun and not by the trigger. I pushed the switch down like you taught me. Mom told me to rest it on the hood of the truck and wait for the guys to come out. When they walked out of the store, I shot them both. When I shot the first guy, he fell into the grocery cart the other one was pushing. It was just like when I shot that fat infected lady that was trying to eat me yesterday."

Connor cringed as Toby paused for a breath. This was exactly what Connor had been trying to protect him from. Nobody should have to take another person's life, especially a boy Toby's age. At the same time, he felt pride that his son was able to do what needed to be done to protect himself and the others from what would have occurred had he not taken the two lives. He would much prefer Toby to live with the guilt rather than have him and Luke brutally murdered and Katie and Eve endure the horrors awaiting them at the hands of Curtis and his crew.

Matt jumped in to finish the story. "Frank was driving us toward the station when we heard a gun popping away further up the road. Instead of turning toward the station, Frank kept going to check out what was happening and see if somebody needed help. We couldn't have been more surprised when we saw Eve and Katie running up the road toward us. Toby was blasting away at infected with the rifle he picked up, while Luke was lighting them up with a flashlight he took from the truck. They made a pretty good team. We uncuffed the girls and came to meet you. When we got here, we saw the Hummer in front and left the girls and kids in the car, fearing the worst. I've got to tell you, it looked pretty bad when we walked into the hall. I thought they got you."

THE FLIGHT

"You know me better than that," Connor said, trying to put up a nonchalant edifice as he thought back to how close he came to losing his fight with Curtis.

Toby was hovering over Connor, still not convinced he wasn't going to die. "I'm going to be okay, Buddy. I'm a little banged up, but I'm going to make it," Connor said, trying to give a reassuring grin. His lips were still oozing blood, which coated his teeth. His attempt at a reassuring grin unsettled Toby even further. Connor pulled Toby to himself, hugging him. Even though it sent a searing pain through his broken rib, Connor squeezed him tighter. "I'm really going to be okay, Son. How are you doing?"

"I want it to go back to how it used to be," Toby said. "I want those things to go away. I want people to stop trying to hurt us." He squeezed Connor's neck tighter as his soft voice grew more and more emotional. His words turned to sobs as his defenses collapsed, leaving the raw emotions of a vulnerable eight year old boy exposed for all to see. His short life had not equipped him with the tools needed to process and cope with the multitude of hopes, fears and pains that had threatened to overwhelm him throughout the last day and a half. No amount of experience could prepare a person for what Toby had gone through.

"Son, I don't know if things will ever go back to the way they used to be. I don't know if the infected will ever go away, either. Whatever happens, our family is going to take care of each other. As long as we have each other, we're going to be okay."

"Toby," Matt said, kneeling down beside him and Connor. "We are going to make it even if life is different than it used to be." Matt stood up and reached down to

Connor. As Connor took his hand, Matt pulled him to his feet. "We need to get out of here and get you cleaned up."

"Mom and Dad have an extra room at their place and somebody can use Jeb's room," Frank said. "We have the bunk house, too. There's room for everybody out there."

An hour later, Connor was toweling water off his battered body after a hot shower. He cautiously lowered himself into bed beside Katie and, without saying a word, instantly drifted off to freedom from lawless, marauding criminals and the infected.

Part 2

Atlanta, Georgia
Thursday Morning

Chapter 7

Zeke immediately noticed two things when he opened his eyes. First, he was lying on his left side, his right thigh pulled up perpendicular to his body with his knee bent at ninety degrees. It was the same position he had assumed just prior to falling asleep. He hadn't moved all night. Second, and more important, he realized the ache that had racked his body for the last two days was completely gone. There was no uncomfortable bloating in his abdomen, no pressure building within his bowels. There was no excessive saliva accumulating in his mouth, signaling the onslaught of another round of vomiting.

He had felt "off" when he left work Monday afternoon. He wasn't really sick; he just didn't feel right. It was a slow day and he had put in six or seven hours at the office over the weekend, so he decided to leave early.

The moment he opened the door to his apartment, he was overcome by the aroma of simmering beans wafting out the door. The smell normally had an effect similar to what Pavlov's bell had on his dogs: instant salivation from the anticipation of food.

But on Monday afternoon, the smell brought on a wave of nausea that he was barely able to suppress. All he could do was unplug his Crock Pot, hurriedly move the beans onto the balcony, and turn on the vent fan above the stove to pull the offending odor out of the apartment before the nausea drove him to his knees in front of the toilet.

The fan didn't have the power to draw the smell out of the apartment in a timely manner. Although he didn't want to, Zeke finally resorted to opening a window and turning on the whole house fan in the hallway. In a matter of minutes, the smell was gone and along with it, the crippling nausea.

The monstrous fan blades created another dilemma, however. Although the fan had effectively removed every vestige of the provoking scent, it could not work in a vacuum. Every liter of air the fan drew from the house had to be replaced with another liter of air from outside. The house was now full of ninety degree air saturated with moisture from the brewing Georgia thunderstorm. The humidity was nearly one hundred percent. Within twenty minutes at most, the charcoal clouds would be thoroughly impregnated with moisture and would begin to vent excess liquid in the form of rain.

The hot, humid air filling his house was almost as bad as the smell of food had been. He quickly closed the window and turned the fan off.

In a continuous motion, he moved his hand to the thermostat and dropped the temperature to fifty-eight degrees. It was as low as it could be set. He intellectually knew setting it at fifty-eight wouldn't cool the house any faster than leaving it at seventy-two where it had been. He also knew fifty-eight would be too cold.

That knowledge didn't matter. All that mattered was sweat was beading on his forehead. It had already soaked through his t-shirt, and was beginning to saturate his dress shirt around the armpits. The muggy air felt like it was suffocating him. Dropping the thermostat to fifty-eight had psychological implications: somehow, it made him feel cooler.

His body suddenly began to ache, as if the hot, damp air had catalyzed some sort of reaction that had been slowly steeping away within his joints. His gut was roiling in discomfort. It felt like part of the storm developing outside had moved inside his belly and was about to reach a crescendo.

In an instant, he knew he only had moments to get his besieged body to the bathroom. Upon his arrival, he couldn't decide whether to raise the seat and kneel before the toilet or leave it in the down position and sit on it instead. In the end, he sat on the seat and picked up the wastebasket resting beside the porcelain throne. Whether the vomiting came first or it was preceded by the diarrhea didn't matter. Either way, one preceded and precipitated the explosive arrival of the other.

After several minutes the attack subsided. Zeke felt like every drop of energy had been wrung from his body. He stepped out of his clothes and left them to lie on the floor while he cleansed his defiled body in a cold shower. By the time he was done, the combination of cold water and the rapid onset of a fever left him chilled to the core and shivering.

His trembling hand reached around the shower door for the towel hanging limply from the wall. Feebly, he struggled to sop the dripping water from his body. He didn't feel like making the effort; however, he knew the remaining water wouldn't evaporate on its own in the high humidity. Once he was dry, he staggered to bed, nestled his naked body between the sheets, and went to sleep.

He was roused from his sleep by a flash and explosion

that rattled the windows as the thunder rumbled away into the distance. Awakened, the turmoil within his bowls intensified and he rushed to the bathroom again. The thunder awakened him several more times, providing just enough warning for him to make it to the safety of the bathroom. Finally, the storm faded away in the cooling night and his innards, in response, seemed to relax for several hours.

Tuesday was a sleep-induced blur punctuated with moments of wakeful terror as he raced for the toilet. Fortunately, each time his body woke him in time to reach the safety of the bathroom. After each desperate race against his body's turmoil, he forced himself to drink as much Gatorade as his body would tolerate and then returned to bed.

Wednesday was more of the same, but by evening he felt he was beginning to recuperate. The vomiting and diarrhea had subsided. His body was slowly winning the battle against the invading virus. His appetite had returned and he considered eating something light. His body had expended a tremendous amount of energy by metabolically raising his temperature in an attempt to cook the besieging virus to death, and it was begging to have its stores replenished. In the end, he decided against it. As famished as he was, he sensed his body would revolt against anything solid he introduced to his digestive tract. Better to wait another day.

He didn't have the energy to do anything other than roll onto his left side and raise his right thigh perpendicular to his body in an attempt to alleviate the discomfort in his stomach. With that laborious task completed, he closed his eyes.

That was how he found himself when he awoke Thursday morning. The difference was that, in spite of his fast-induced weakened state, he felt great.

Chapter 8

Zeke didn't move for several minutes. He lay beneath the covers, reveling in the fact that he wasn't sick anymore. During the past two days, he had forgotten what it was like to feel well.

It was the persistent, gnawing hunger that finally drove him from his bed. He hadn't eaten for two and a half days and desperately needed sustenance. He tossed the blankets off and pushed himself off the mattress. His frame was grasped by the chill air in the room, and goose bumps sprouted all over his body while he fumbled to dress himself. Although the fifty-eight degree air was invigorating, it was economically unfeasible to keep the temperature that cold, especially during the summer. Bumping the thermostat back up to seventy-two degrees, Zeke shuddered as he pondered how much he was going to have to shell out in exchange for having dropped the temperature low enough to keep milk from spoiling.

Breakfast was basically the same every day: four eggs beaten and cooked into an omelet topped with cheddar cheese and served beside a piece of toast drenched in butter.

Zeke knew that his body had cannibalized a lot of muscle while he lay in bed without eating. He was anxious to refuel with the protein the eggs would provide. He anguished at the thought of the muscle that had melted away. It wasn't that he was particularly vain about his physique. It had more to do with the hours he worked to acquire it.

There would be no working out today. It was already seven and he always tried to get to work by eight even though the office didn't officially open until nine. With traffic, it would probably take forty minutes get there. He hadn't planned on going to work at all, but he felt so good there was no point in staying home another day. His friends said he was a workaholic, and they were probably right.

After breakfast, he took a quick shower and threw on his work attire. It was seven-twenty. If there weren't any accidents along the way, he would make it by eight. He locked the door and bounded down the concrete stairs two at a time. Breakfast had renewed his vigor and put energy back in his step. He felt good.

The steps from his second story apartment dropped him onto the broom-finished sidewalk that led to the car port. He could never figure out the appeal of broom-finished concrete. It would probably be okay in North Dakota where the sidewalks were frozen eight months a year, but traction wasn't an issue in Georgia. He couldn't remember the last time the sidewalk had ice for even a couple hours during the day.

When he rounded the corner of the building and came into view of the covered carport, he was surprised to see that it was nearly full. By this time on a weekday, at least half of the slots were normally empty. He looked at his watch to make sure it wasn't the weekend. The watch indicated it was Thursday. To the best of his recollection,

THE FLIGHT

May 15th wasn't more important than any other day of the year. There was no reason people would have the day off. With a shrug, he pushed the unlock button on his remote and was greeted by the brief illumination of every light on his F-150.

At the firm where he worked, a seven series Beamer was considered an entry level car and Bentleys were commonplace. At first, stuffy co-workers frowned at his six year old pickup; it didn't fit the image they were all scrambling to portray. It didn't scream wealth like their hundred thousand dollar rides. His apartment didn't fit the bill either, by a factor of at least ten. He made a lot of money, enough to have easily paid cash for a big house in a good neighborhood as well as a luxury car to park in front of it. Those things didn't matter to him.

His job and money were a means to an end that he was striving to achieve. He was saving to buy a ranch in Wyoming and not have to worry whether or not it made a profit. To that end, he lived as cheaply as he possibly could. He would happily forgo a luxurious lifestyle that didn't appeal to him today in order to achieve a different lifestyle that did appeal to him down the road.

A mile from his house, Zeke hit the freeway. It was empty, with only a handful of cars going into the city. The lanes out of the city were a different situation, though. A solid stream of cars was leaving Atlanta; at least six or seven times the normal traffic volume was crawling out of the city toward the suburbs. It was exactly the opposite of how it should be. He knew he was missing something and reached to turn on the radio. He stopped short of the empty hole in the dash, remembering his truck had been broken into four days prior. Why somebody would take a stock Ford radio was beyond him. Zeke would have to wait until he got to work to figure out what was happening.

The closer to the city he got, the heavier traffic leaving the city became. Like a lemming, he considered getting off the freeway and joining the exodus to the suburbs, but his thoughts were interrupted by the scream of a siren behind him. Before he could look in the mirror, a wall of air rocked his truck and pushed it to the side of his lane as a column of eight Dodge Chargers, painted in the blue and silver of the Georgia State Patrol, blasted past him at what must have been one hundred and forty miles per hour. At the seventy miles per hour he had set the cruise control, they literally passed him like he wasn't moving.

Zeke had always been drawn to danger and excitement. He had nearly followed his older brother, Connor, into law enforcement to chase adrenaline rushes, but in college, when he discovered his uncanny ability to predict trends in the stock market, he went into investments instead. When he listened to his brother's stories, he sometimes regretted his decision, but it was a means to an end; it was taking him closer to the ranch in Wyoming.

He decided to continue on to his office at the edge of downtown unless he saw a convincing reason to turn back. He wouldn't panic and mindlessly flee the city simply because others did. By the time he reached his exit, twelve more patrol cars had blasted past him in ones, twos and groups of three. Something big was going on. After the last group of three cars blew by, he slammed his fist down on the top of the steering wheel, frustrated by not knowing what was happening. As he was envisioning crushing the nose of the thief who stole his radio, a horn honked behind him from one of the few cars going into the city. He looked up and realized the light at the end of the off ramp had turned to green.

As he worked his way through the maze of city streets to his office, he noticed that only a small fraction of the normal pedestrian traffic hurried along the sidewalks, and the few people he saw were all moving with a purpose. Everyone had their head on a swivel, looking around nervously as they hastily made their way to their destinations.

As Zeke neared his office in the financial district, the image of his truck glided smoothly across the spotless surface of the mirrored glass fronting the buildings on either side of the street. As he proceeded west, the buildings decreased from fifteen stories to an average of four. He made a right turn, followed by an immediate left into the drive that descended into the parking garage beneath his office.

Stopping at the horizontal arm with his work ID in hand, he waited for the parking attendant to raise the gate and admit him into the garage. It took a couple seconds to realize nobody was in the booth. He waited for a minute and grew impatient. He opened his door, stepped onto the concrete drive, and walked around back of the security booth. Pushing through the unlatched door, he quickly located a green button marked "Raise Arm." He pressed the button and heard the quiet whir of an electric motor spinning outside as the arm briskly rose.

Zeke hastily reentered his truck and proceeded down the ramp into the bowels of the garage. The subterranean parking structure was the antithesis of the parking lot at his apartment: it was nearly empty. A handful of cars ranging from low-end compacts to mid-priced sedans were congregated just outside the reserved spots flanking the stairwell and elevator shaft. None of the reserved spaces were occupied. Normally by this time in the morning, at least four or five of the partners in the firm were already at work. Today none of them were present. As he pulled into his reserved parking place, Zeke's curiosity continued to swell. Something major was going on if none of the other partners had arrived by 7:50.

Chapter 9

Zeke reached the top of the drab concrete stairwell and stepped through the metal door, passing into the reception area. The contrast between the utilitarian stairwell from the basement and the marble floor and dark walnut paneling of the reception was so stark, new clients often stopped and stared when they entered the building for the first time.

It was no surprise to Zeke that neither the night guard nor the receptionist was behind the speckled granite top of the reception counter. This morning, nothing seemed to be as it should. He walked around the alcove and pushed through the nine foot oak doors that led to the offices. He looked into the dark interior of each conference room and office he passed as he plodded down the hallway, the thick, plush carpet silencing each footfall.

The first floor was empty, with no indication anybody had been there recently. Even the coffee pot in the big conference room was cold.

Rather than walk back into the reception area to ride the elevator to the second floor, Zeke took the stairs at the end of the hall. Unlike the stairwell from the basement, the interior stairwell was richly decorated.

Zeke paused at the second floor landing, hesitant to confirm his suspicion that he was alone in the building. He knew most of his colleagues would have come to work from their death beds. His curiosity about the mass exodus from the city and the mystery of his absent co-workers overcame his apprehensions. He pulled the tall oak door in toward the stairwell and entered the hallway that formed a ring inside second floor offices. More importantly, it led to the break room with cable TV.

Entering the hallway, Zeke immediately heard a voice coming from ahead and around the corner. He quickly traversed the length of the hall and made the right turn. His step was quickened by light spilling through the doorway of the break room and the female voice speaking excitedly within the room.

When he entered the room, Zeke's mounting uneasiness initially began to subside at the sight of six people. They had moved chairs away from the table and arranged them in a haphazard semicircle around the television hanging in the corner of the room. All eyes were riveted to the screen as if it were a magician about to perform a sleight of hand trick. Nobody turned to acknowledge him. Nobody spoke. Nobody moved. They sat transfixed, staring at the screen.

When Zeke moved far enough into the room to see the screen, the image he saw froze him where he stood as dread trickled into the center of his stomach.

The scenes flashing in the box in the top right corner of the screen looked like images from a movie, except the television was tuned to Fox News. The female voice he had heard in the hall was from the commentator. Her tightly drawn face indicated this wasn't an entertainment exposé about a newly released blockbuster. The near panic in her voice reflected the seriousness of whatever was occurring on the screen.

The scene from the box inset in the corner of the screen

enlarged, replacing the commentator. At full screen, the grisly details emerged. On a street in an unidentified city, buildings on the right side of the screen were fully engulfed in flames as was a car on the side of the street. But that was not the focus of the shot. The focus was on the street itself. A dozen or so people were running toward the camera, dropping purses and other personal effects as they ran. The audio was still from the commentator. It was clear many of the fleeing people were screaming as they fled past the camera with mouths open and faces full of terror.

The camera then focused down the street. Half a dozen bodies lay randomly in the road. A handful of people were tending to the seemingly unconscious forms in the street.

The camera zoomed in until it included only a single prostrate body with two good Samaritans beside it. One was on his knees facing the camera and the other was bent over the body, which was lying on its back. The blurry image suddenly came into focus. The man on his knees, facing the camera, was covered in blood. A crimson flood had poured from his mouth and down his white shirt.

Zeke's mouth opened as he wondered how a person so wounded could tend to another. As he wondered, the battered man knelt down toward the unconscious victim of whatever tragedy was being displayed. His face disappeared behind the second person who was knelt over the unconscious form and was facing away from the camera. The body facing away from the camera slowly stood up and turned into view. The woman's face was covered in blood, like the other, but her mouth was opening and closing in what Zeke recognized as chewing. The camera moved back to the victim on the road. When the female moved to the side, the ghastly scene became clear. Zeke's stomach turned when he realized the man wasn't helping the victim on the ground, but was tearing flesh from the body with his teeth. The blood running down his face and shirt wasn't his own; it was from the body in the road. When he stood up, pieces of flesh adhered to his mustache. He followed the woman and they joined another defiled figure and began tearing at a squirming body laying supine on the asphalt surface.

The scene rendered Zeke as speechless as the rest of the group. He was hypnotized by the carnage he was seeing. As disturbing as it was, he couldn't break his eyes free from the barbaric spectacle in front of him.

When the initial shock of the sight subsided enough for Zeke to regain his senses, he focused on the commenter's voice.

"This scene from Los Angeles is being replayed in cities and towns all across the western United States," she said. "It began with this footage from security cameras in the Reno Airport late yesterday afternoon," she added as the scene from the street was replaced by a black and white video of a woman lying on a bed in what appeared to be a first aid station.

Beside the woman, whose face was bloodied, two boys in a similar condition lay on two other beds. "This woman and the two boys apparently had seizures and died in the Reno Airport. About thirty minutes later, this occurred."

As the commentator spoke, the woman's right hand began to move. Then her chest began heaving as if she were trying to regain her breath. Within seconds she sat up, looked around, and then pivoted her legs off the bed. At the same time, the door into the room opened and a female nurse entered, stopping when she came face to face with the patient, who was now on her feet. The newcomer slowly backed out the doorway with a puzzled look on her face. The woman from the bed lunged toward the door.

The scene cut to a new view from a camera in the adjoining room, showing a rear view of the woman backing out of the room. She was suddenly tackled as the woman from the bed flew through the doorway, knocking her over and landing on top of her. Attacking, the woman lowered her head to the nurse's throat. When the head came back up, a black and white geyser erupted from the nurse. The blood spray covered the attacker as her face returned to the nurse's neck. A man suddenly entered another door into the room, probably drawn by the screams. The woman from the bed rose upright, forgetting the nurse on the ground, as she pursued the fleeing man.

The picture switched to another camera showing a view within the terminal. The woman from the bed pursued the man into the scene. People fled in all directions at the appearance of the crazed, bloody woman. Her attention was diverted from the man to a female traveler who stood frozen in terror.

The scene from the second room replayed as the woman from the bed pounced on the traveler, sending her rolling carryon bag skidding across the floor. A man ran across the seating area of the terminal and attempted to pull the crazed woman off the person she was attacking.

But her focus could not be broken even as the man grabbed both arms from behind and wrenched her from the victim on the floor. With a violent lunge forward, the attacker broke free of his grip and fell back on top of the traveler who was still on the floor. The man lost his balance and reeled backward, sprawling onto the tile, momentarily leaving the victim without a defender. The attacker's face dove for the tender neck beneath her. Even the silent, black and white nature of the video couldn't mask the terror that was unfolding in the scene as a dark pool ebbed across the floor from beneath the two women.

The man rose to his feet and renewed his attempt to pull the attacker from the woman as three more men ran to his aid. The attacker diverted her attention from the victim beneath her and twisted within the grasp of the man. The woman on the floor clutched at her throat with both hands and darkness spread from between her fingers as they were doused in the blood rushing freely from her wound.

The attacking woman quickly overwhelmed the man, knocking him to his back. As she dove on top of him, he wrapped his hands around her neck, barely keeping her gaping maw at bay. Her hands battered him as her teeth opened and closed inches from his exposed neck. It appeared that hope was lost until the three men reached the grappling battle.

Two men reached her in unison, each grabbing one of her arms and pulling her off the man on the ground. As they pulled her backwards, the third man grabbed one of her legs. The man on the ground quickly pulled himself erect and grabbed her other leg.

The woman kicked violently as she struggled to escape the clutches of the attacking quartet. Each time she lashed out with a foot, the man attached to her leg struggled desperately to maintain his hold.

The television switched to a split screen with one half showing the battle in the terminal and the other showing the first aid room. Zeke didn't understand why until he realized that one of the boys was starting to move. His chest began heaving and he suddenly sat upright, swung his feet to the floor, and walked out the door. The right side of the picture switched to the second camera as the boy entered its field of view.

He stopped when he reached the corpse on the floor. His head tilted sideways and his teeth opened and closed silently as he looked at the body, his face full of longing. Then his attention was instantly drawn to the open doorway leading into the terminal.

The boy's head began bobbing up and down rigidly and he suddenly broke into a run. The image returned to the full screen shot from the camera in the terminal showing the boy running spastically, head bobbing, toward the melee on the floor.

Three more men had joined the fracas. The woman was now on her back bucking violently against the four men who were holding her arms down. Two of the original men were still hanging onto her jerking and kicking legs and the seventh man sat astride her torso with his hands wrapped around her neck, trying to hold her thrashing head against the floor.

Nobody engaged in the struggle to subdue the woman noticed the approaching boy until he lunged into the man holding her right leg and sent him sprawling into the man holding the left. With her legs free, the woman bucked her torso up, causing the man astride her abdomen to lose his balance and collapse forward, where her awaiting mouth clamped shut on his cheek. Her head twisted, biting off a chunk of his face. He rolled off clutching his cheek with both hands.

One of the two guys restraining her left arm turned his

attention to the boy who was now attacking the men he had just sent sprawling. They were trying to disentangle themselves from each other while futilely attempting to fight off the boy. The scene of chaos descended into pandemonium.

And then the second boy erupted through the door and into the terminal. His entrance wasn't noticed until he pounced onto the back of one of the men holding the woman's right arm down. The two men remaining were unable to control her and the tide of the struggle turned for the third time. Now it was in favor of the woman and the boys.

The man with the bite torn from his cheek was out of the fight, leaving two men for each of the attackers. Even through the younger of the boys appeared to be only eleven or twelve years old, he easily outmatched the two men before him. In less than twenty seconds, the fight was over. All seven men lay on the floor in broken, battered heaps. The lack of color softened the carnage, but the dark spatters and pools could not be confused with anything besides blood.

It was a massacre.

Chapter 10

The woman and two boys began to feast on the bodies before them. The banquet was interrupted as three police officers entered the screen with guns drawn. The woman looked up and hesitated for a moment, torn between the ample food before her and the prospect of more food fifty feet away.

The officers spread out as they hesitantly drew closer.

As with all predators, the prospect of a living quarry won out. She rose upright and canted her head sideways, looking at the officer in the center. A moment later, she charged.

Still crouched on their haunches, the two boys watched as the center officer's gun bounced in his hands, the recoil from each shot kicking the barrel up. The woman staggered momentarily, but continued her charge, quickly closing the distance. The end of the pistol continued to bounce up and down as the officer rapidly pulled the trigger. Each bounce resulted in the woman jerking as a bullet ripped through her flesh, but still she continued her onslaught. The officer must have emptied his gun because he dropped a hand to the magazine pouch on his belt. He was too late. The woman launched her body, bowling him over.

One of the partner officers bolted to his fallen comrade. He screwed the end of his gun to the side of her head as she tore into the prostrate policeman. An effusion erupted from the opposite side of her head as she slumped to the ground and lay motionless, her body draped across the dead constable beneath her.

The boys lost interest in the feast in front of them. Both rose to their feet and advanced on the officer who had slain the woman. Whether their advance was due to anger over the woman's death, an instinctual response to food, or out of self-preservation was unclear. Whatever the motivation, they charged at full speed. The second officer's gun barrel began bouncing up and down on the television screen as the duo closed the distance to his partner. The third officer lifted his gun, but it didn't recoil immediately. When it did, the older boy's head rocked backwards. His feet stopped moving and his body crumpled to the ground, skidding to a stop. The second boy lunged at the officer, leaving his feet in a flying tackle. At the last moment, the officer moved to the side with the agility of a rodeo clown sidestepping a two thousand pound bull. His gun tracked the body as it crashed down and slid across the tile floor.

The boy immediately pushed himself up on his hands and knees and redirected his attack as he came to his feet. But before he was completely upright, the officer's gun jumped a final time. The boy's head popped back in response to the violent collision of lead and bone. He sank to his knees and slumped backwards to the floor.

The officers shifted their guns from one corpse to the next as if they expected them to rise again and continue their offensive. After several seconds, one officer looked at the other. A moment later the first nodded his head. The second officer holstered his pistol and turned to his fallen partner while the other kept the three bodies covered with his weapon. Seconds later, another officer burst onto the screen. Two more appeared ten seconds later. Within a minute, the screen was filled with officers milling back and forth, most congregated around their fallen brother. A backdrop of spectators gathered behind, looking on in horror.

The screen returned to the commentator who had remained silent during the scene in the airport. She understood the power of letting the video speak for itself. With the recording concluded, she resumed speaking.

"The uncensored carnage you have just witnessed is not isolated to the airport. It has been spreading across the country, popping up here and there in isolated incidents which are growing more and more frequent. People all over the United States are coming down with a mystery illness. Within hours, the virus proves to be fatal. On an average of thirty minutes later, the dead are coming back to life as you have just witnessed.

"Early reports are indicating that these outbreaks of violence are caused by a highly contagious disease. So far every reported case has led to death.

"Additional reports are stating that the only way to stop the infected is to inflict massive head trauma. Officials are advising that everybody avoid the infected at all costs.

"If someone you know becomes infected, notify the police and immediately get away from him. We are being asked to advise the public to stay where they are. If you are at home, stay there. If you are at work, remain there. We don't have official confirmation, but unofficially the sickness is airborne and is highly contagious.

"Coming up next will be Doctor Clark at the Centers for Disease Control. He will fill us in on the details of the infection and recommend precautions against it." The image on the screen returned to video of violence and carnage from across the country. All the clips showed the infected attacking and ravaging terrified citizens.

Chapter 11

Zeke stood motionless for five minutes, spellbound by the images of death and mutilation flashing across the screen. Although the droning of the commentator's voice filled his ears, he didn't register what was being said. Her words had no meaning to him. He was so disturbingly drawn into the visual stimulus, the audio was lost. Finally, he broke free from the hypnotic trance that had held him and looked at the others. None of them had spoken. They, too, were in a state of mesmerized hypnosis.

Zeke hesitated, afraid to speak, almost as if doing so would break some unknown etiquette. Finally the words came out, shaky and unsure, which was unusual for him. "Is the disease here?" he asked.

Meagan, the receptionist, turned, noticing him for the first time since he walked into the room. "I don't know," she said hesitantly. "It sounds like it's everywhere, but they haven't specifically said anything about Atlanta. I came in ten minutes ago, for coffee. They may have said something about it before I got here."

"It's here," James said, without turning away from the screen. James was a broker who had been with the company for about a year. "Before Meagan came in, they put up a map of the country with reported cases shown as red dots. It isn't as bad here as on the west coast because they are quarantining people from the flights that landed last night, but a few flights landed before the quarantine went into effect. As of a couple hours ago, they shut down air travel, and most states have put up roadblocks along their borders."

"Do they think they can contain it?" Zeke asked hopefully.

"I don't know," James stated flatly. "They say they're trying, but who knows. There hasn't been much information at this point. It's caused by some sort of disease, but beyond that, they either don't know or won't say. Some people are saying it's a virus, some are saying it's a bacterial infection. Others are saying it is a terrorist chemical attack. My impression is nobody knows what's causing it. The only thing everybody seems to be agreeing on is that it's best to stay wherever you are."

The screen changed to a small stage with blue curtains in the background. A man with thinning gray hair approached an oak podium emblazoned with a blue graphic containing the letters CDC. His wrinkled button-down shirt and the puffy, dark colored skin behind his large frame glasses suggested he hadn't slept last night, or if he had, he had slept in his cloths and hadn't gotten much rest.

"Good morning." he said, as he placed a sheet of notes on the podium. "My name is Dr. Clark, and I work with the Centers for Disease Control. As you all know, we are faced with an unprecedented situation. A devastating virus is currently sweeping across the nation. The death toll is rising at an exponential rate. There are many things about the virus that are unknown. What we do know is the virus is airborne and is extremely virulent. Current figures are showing that the virus is fatal within six hours of exposure. As many of you have seen in news reports, those who die from the disease are coming back to life approximately thirty minutes after death occurs.

"There are some precautions we are recommending that people take. First of all, stay where you are. If you are at home, do not leave your house. If you happen to be at work, stay there. The best way to protect yourself and your loved ones from the virus is to prevent exposure to it in the first place. We are asking people to remain calm. Panic will not help the situation.

"If you come in contact with someone who is infected, we ask that you notify the nearest hospital and quarantine yourself for at least six hours. Do not go to the hospital because, as of right now, there is nothing they can do for you and you are going to risk exposing large numbers of people.

"People who succumb to the illness and come back from the dead are easy to recognize. They move very erratically. They are unable to speak and their cognitive abilities are decreased to an instinctual level. If you see such a person, notify the police and stay away from the individual. They are extremely aggressive and, as you have probably already seen, will attack without any provocation.

"We don't know a lot about the revived dead, but we do know that they undergo drastic metabolic changes. The only certain way to stop them is to destroy their brain. We are not advocating that people begin hunting the revived dead, but if you encounter one and are forced to defend yourself, injuries that would kill a normal human being have no effect. The infected are able to function indefinitely without their lungs. We believe they need their heart, but even destroying the heart does not produce immediate death. It is believed that they can live for upwards of twenty minutes without a beating heart.

"I am not going to take questions at this time. We will be making regular statements when more information is available. At this point, all I can say is stay where you are."

As Dr. Clark folded his notes and placed them in his pocket, the reporters in the room exploded in a raucous uproar of questions that prevented any one individual from being heard.

Dr. Clark raised his hand and the room quieted. "I will make another statement as soon as there is more to tell."

As he turned to walk away, a booming voice erupted before it could be covered by the others. "Doctor, how bad is it?" the man asked.

Dr. Clark stopped mid-stride and turned back to the sea of reporters. "It is the worst case scenario we could have imagined. It is imperative that you shelter in place. Stay where you are." And he walked off the stage, disappearing behind the curtain, chased by the din of questions reverberating through the room.

Chapter 12

The broadcast on the television returned to the commentator. Apparently, Dr. Clark's speech had the same effect on her as it had on the viewers in the break room. She sat silent for several seconds before she started. "We have just heard Dr. Clark at the CDC shed some light on what is happening. We learned the infection is caused by a virus. Dr. Clark has advised everyone to take shelter wherever they are. It is your best hope to avoid contact with what we are learning is a highly contagious disease." Even the studio makeup and lighting couldn't hide the pallor that washed over her skin. She had lost the objectivity and indifference newscasters strive so hard to portray. She had just as much at stake as the viewers. She was susceptible to the same fears and emotions as everybody else, and she had reached the limit of what she could hide.

In an uncharacteristic act of vulnerability, she turned to the side and asked, "Could somebody please bring me some water?" A young woman quickly and self-consciously walked onto the set with a clear plastic bottle and set it on the desk before scurrying out of view. The anchor twisted the top and chugged half the bottle before recapping it and setting it out of view below the desk. She continued speaking, obviously disturbed.

Bruce, who was sitting at the right side of the ring of chairs, turned and asked, "What do we do?"

"Do whatever you want," James said as he stood up. "I'm out of here, though. I'm going home to get my wife and we're heading to our cabin in Blairsville. We don't have a lot of room, but anyone who needs a place can come with us. We have plenty of food there and we have a well with good water on the property."

"But they said to stay where we are," Meagan interrupted.

"I'm not begging you to come. I'm just offering an out of the way place to hide out," James retorted. "Do whatever you want. I don't care. What about you?" he asked, turning to face Zeke.

"I don't know." Zeke hesitated. "Blairsville is a two hour drive on a good day. Traffic was really heavy leaving town when I came in. With the announcement we just heard, it's going to be gridlock. I appreciate the offer, but I think I like my chances here in the building. There's food and water and we can lock up and stay secure. I'm afraid it's going to be anarchy out there."

"All right," James said as he started for the door. "Anybody else want to come?" Several people shook their heads no, while others simply stared at the floor, wondering if they were doing the right thing by passing on a place to escape outside of the city. "Good luck to all of you," he said as he walked out the door.

"Wait a minute," Bruce said, standing up. "I'm coming with you." He nearly toppled his chair in his haste to not be left behind.

After the two left the room, Zeke turned his back to the

TV and the others in the room and walked to the window which overlooked the empty street. Looking as far as possible in either direction, he saw no one except an old bum burrowing through a trash can. After several minutes, James's Infinity pull out of the side street and start east toward the freeway.

"Why don't you turn it to a local station and see what's happening here?" someone suggested. The local situation was different, but not better. Five minutes was enough for Zeke to realize he should have turned around before he made it to work. The clips didn't show the infected mauling people. Instead it showed healthy people looting and mugging other people. Gangs were leaving their neighborhoods in mass, having already plundered the local stores. Moving to higher-end shopping centers, they were killing anyone who got in their way and walking out with whatever they could carry.

Scenes from grocery stores were just as bad. Soccer moms were heaping weeks' worth of food into over laden carts and simply pushing past objecting employees without paying. Mini vans were exiting the premises with groceries stacked up to the windows. Within half an hour of the CDC announcement, shelves were picked clean of anything useful. Many owners simply refused to open the doors of their businesses. Armed guards for hire became the top commodity in the city. They defended businesses until somebody with a bigger gun wanted to shop. A lone man could do little against a determined, armed mob.

There seemed to be a unanimous sentiment that leaving the city was a good thing. Those who had cars hit the freeway. Bus drivers absconded with city buses and began offering high-dollar, overcrowded rides out of the city to anyone who would pay.

A taxi ride that cost eighty dollars yesterday cost a thousand today, cash up front. The freeways became impassable. Rather than wait an hour to fill up with gas, people tried to make it out of the city on fumes and ran out of fuel. Even if they could have moved to the shoulder, it wouldn't have mattered because the shoulder had become another lane of travel. People simply left their dead cars in the lane, and began walking. Lanes into the city became lanes out of the city, but it made no difference because they plugged up, too.

City streets fared no better. Any street with a gas station had lines half a mile long or more, effectively preventing any through traffic.

The police were out in force, but they could only do so much. They began responding in groups of four. 911 lines were inundated to the point that calling was of no use. Units were self-dispatched by the sound of gun fire rather than the radio. Looting was overlooked so long as it occurred peacefully, and more than one clip showed on-duty officers themselves looting. For the most part, though, law enforcement efforts were focused on keeping the gangs and general anarchy in check, and they seemed to be effective to some degree.

"I don't understand," Meagan said, looking out the window. "The TV says the roads are all blocked, but there isn't a single car on this one."

"It's because there's nothing of value on this street," one of the IT guys said. "We're in the financial district and the road doesn't go anywhere. There's no reason for anybody to be here."

"He's right," Zeke agreed. "This is probably one of the

safest places in the city. I can't think of any reason people would come here."

Chapter 13

Twice during the morning, low riders with dark tint blazed past the building with police cars close behind, mirroring their movement through the city, their sirens screaming like spoiled children.

After watching the news for another hour, Zeke couldn't take anymore. The only things that changed were the rising death toll and the escalating violence.

The IT guy, whose name was John, suggested that they split up and take inventory of anything in the building that could be of use. The food on hand would determine how long they could remain in the building before they were forced to leave in search of supplies.

Everybody agreed and they split up into two groups. Zeke, Meagan, and the building maintenance guy, Mike, took the top two floors. John, and L.C., the security guard, agreed to inventory the bottom two floors.

After thirty minutes, the group reassembled in the break room. Between the cafe on the fourth floor, the vending machines in the break room, and food people had stashed in their offices, they figured they could comfortably last for a week and a half to two weeks before they had to begin searching for food.

The afternoon slowly dragged into evening with the five remaining holdouts glued to the television. Dr. Clark from the CDC came on numerous times, but didn't have anything useful to add to his first announcement.

Around ten, L.C. asked if anyone minded if he changed the channel back to Fox News. Nobody cared. The local station was mostly carrying the network coverage anyway. There was very little local information. L.C. rapidly clicked through a handful of variety channels before he settled in on Fox News.

On the screen was a studio shot with a male anchor talking. "A source has identified the woman and boys from the incident at the Reno Airport as Claire Mantell. The two boys were her sons. Our source has reported that she was from the small town of Lost Hills, California, where we are told the outbreak began yesterday afternoon."

"Did he just say Lost Hills?" Zeke asked in alarm.

"Yeah," John said, still focused on the screen. "Why?"

"My brother Connor lives there," Zeke stated flatly as he dug his cell phone out of his pocket and tapped out a phone number on the touch screen. He was greeted by a recorded message telling him all cell circuits were busy. Zeke moved to the phone hanging on the wall and punched the same numbers on the dial pad.

After three rings, an apprehensive voice answered, "Hello."

"Connor, I didn't figure you were still alive," Zeke responded. "I just heard that all this started under your watch."

"Sorry to disappoint you," answered the voice on the other end of a bad connection. "I'm still alive and you're still going to have to split Mom and Dad's stuff with me when they croak," the voice said with a laugh. "I do have some good news for you though. You're immune to the infection. I don't have time to explain it right now, but you're going to be okay in that regard."

Zeke paused for several seconds before he responded. "How could you know that I'm immune?" he questioned.

"Like I said, I don't have time to explain it, but trust me, you are. I have three guys waiting for me to get off the phone so I can't talk long. How are things in Atlanta?" Connor asked.

"They're bad, really bad. There are quite a few infected running around. The real problem is with the uninfected, though. The gangs are robbing, looting, and killing with impunity. This morning the police were keeping them at bay. By late afternoon, I think most of the cops had bugged out. I haven't seen any law enforcement outside the office for a couple hours."

"You're still at work? Why?" Connor prodded. "The financial system is ruined. Nobody's going to be worried about their 401Ks today. You haven't had a buy or sell order all day, have you?"

"I didn't watch the news this morning. I got to work and only a few people showed up. By the time I realized I needed to get out of the city, it was too late. I figured I would be safer waiting it out in the office than trying to navigate the streets."

Connor interrupted. "I don't care what's going on in the streets. You have to get out of the city. Now! The infection will spread faster there than it has here. I've seen over ten percent of our population infected in about twenty four hours. That only includes what I have seen with my own eyes, not the ones locked in their houses. Once they fill the streets in Atlanta, you won't stand a chance of getting out."

"We're pretty safe here," Zeke said. "We have a week and a half or two weeks of food in the building. We're going to stay here until we have to leave for more. Hopefully the roads will have opened up by then. Right now they're too congested to drive."

"Zeke, you aren't listening to me." Connor said, with irritation thick in his voice. "Once the population turns, you won't be able to get out of the city. I thought the infection could be contained. It can't. So far all it's done in Lost Hills is spread exponentially. You have to leave before the population's infected."

"I don't know," Zeke countered. "Everyone on TV is saying to stay where you are."

"That might be the best way to avoid exposure, but when your food runs out, you're going to have to leave your building to get more. You guys are going to be ripped apart by the infected once you have to leave your building.

"The local doctor here is friends with a big wig at the CDC who told my him that when the Chinese were doing experiments with city sized populations, the infected killed everybody who wasn't infected. Your only chance is to get out of Atlanta and find a place with no people around."

"Okay," Zeke conceded. "I'll talk it over with the people here and see what we're going to do."

"Talk it over with them, but you have to leave regardless of what the rest decide to do. Once the infection has run its course through the city, you won't make it out. You have to leave now."

"Alright," Zeke said in frustration. "I'll leave." Although a vestige of adolescent sibling rivalry left him slightly irritated at having to admit his older brother was right, he could see the logic in what Connor was telling him.

"What's the situation out there? Do you have a safe place away from people?"

"For the time being," Connor said. "But that could change in a hurry. You're not thinking of coming out here, are you?"

"If you're right and this is the end, I have to get to a safe place somewhere. Other than a job that apparently isn't going to be around tomorrow, I don't have anything holding me here. Based on what you just told me, I'm going to try to get home. I haven't been able to reach Mom and Dad, but that's where I'm going to head. If things end up as bad as you're making them out, we're going to need to stick together. Are you going home?"

"I would like to, but I can't. These people have entrusted me with protecting them. I can't leave them when they need me the most."

"Are you seriously going try to make it from Georgia to California?" Connor questioned, pondering the enormity of the task Zeke was suggesting. It was a solid three day drive under the best of conditions. These weren't even going to be marginal conditions.

Zeke paused for several seconds as he considered the proposition to which he had just committed himself. "I don't know how it's going to work out, but I can't stay here after what I just learned. Is there anything else I should know before I start?"

"Not much that I can think of. Make sure your friends wear some sort of masks. I don't know how effective they are, but it's better than nothing. Do you have any weapons?"

"I have a pistol in my truck with two extra clips."

"Okay, that's good." Connor paused, encouraged by the unexpected news that his younger brother was armed. "If you have to shoot, aim for the head. Body shots are completely ineffective. Three magazines won't last long as things start to get worse. Try to find a rifle. Move quietly and get out of the city as fast as you can. I wish I could tell you something more helpful."

"Look," Zeke said, and paused. His changed tone told Connor what was coming. "I know my chances of making it across the country are slim at best." Zeke's voice filled with emotion as he continued. "If I don't make it, take care of your family and Mom and Dad, too."

"You'll make it," Connor said, trying to reassure himself as much as Zeke. "Be careful and stay in touch. Call me tomorrow. Text if I don't answer. I wish I had more time, but I have to go." Zeke pulled the receiver from his ear and eyed it for several seconds before placing it back in the cradle.

"Who was that?" Meagan questioned. She had been eyeing him during the entire phone conversation.

"It was my brother," Zeke answered slowly, thinking of the cross country trip he had committed himself to undertaking.

"Oh," she said softly. "Are you leaving us to go to him?" she asked as tears began welling up along the edges of her lower eyelids.

"Yes, I'm going to try to get home to my family. My brother lives in Lost Hills where the infection started. My parents live a couple hours away from there." Zeke relayed what his brother, Connor, had told him about the infection rates in Lost Hills. "He lives in a very isolated, rural area. If the infection is spreading that fast where he lives, it's going to be a hundred times as bad here. If we don't get out of the city before the infection starts spreading here, we won't be able to get out. If we had to, we could probably make our food here stretch for three weeks, but after that, we're going to have to leave the building. Either way, we're going to have to leave at some point."

"He's right," L.C. agreed with a sigh. "We have a better chance of getting out now rather than later."

"Where can we go?" Meagan asked as tears began streaming from her eyes. "They told us to stay where we are. I can't get home. There's more food here than at my house anyway. We can't leave." Her breaths came in gulps and her body shook as her weeping turned to sobbing.

Zeke walked across the room and wrapped his arms around her as she buried her head in his shoulder. It was an unnatural gesture for him as he was uncomfortable around emotional women. His instinct was to shun her, but he forced himself to push through his comfort zone. He could tell she was on the verge of a breakdown and, in this instance, he could understand why. He was coping with the stress better than she was, but he could still feel its crushing weight pushing in on him. The debilitating panic was rising up within himself as well. If they were going to leave, they couldn't afford her panicking or losing control. Survival depended on everybody pulling his own weight.

"Everyone is going to have to decide the best course of action for himself," Zeke said. As a partner in the company, he was the *de facto* leader of the group. "Everybody here has family and friends they are concerned about and want to be with. I'm going to Northern

California where my family is. They have a farm and a climate with a long growing season. They live a few miles out of a small town. It's a good place to survive if things get worse. If any of you want to, you're welcome to come with me. It's going to be a long trip and I honestly don't know if I'll be able to get there, but I'm leaving as soon as I can get my truck loaded up."

Meagan pulled away, looking into Zeke's face as she did. "I didn't say anything earlier, but my sister sent me a text a couple hours ago. My mom has the sickness. I can't go to them. My sister and dad are going to get it, too." Her voice broke back into sobs until she regained enough composure to continue. "I want to come with you. I don't have anywhere else to go," she finally succeeded in getting out.

"Of course you can come with me," Zeke said reassuringly, though he silently dreaded the prospect of taking Meagan with him. It wasn't that he didn't like her, because he did. She was normally a cheerful and bubbly person. Everybody liked her. His problem was that she was going to be an anchor. She had little, if anything, to contribute and was going to slow him down, but like she said, she didn't have anywhere else to go, and he knew she wouldn't survive on her own.

"Anybody else want to come with me?" he asked, looking around the room.

"Not me," John said as he met Zeke's gaze. "I have my wife and kids at home. I was going to have them meet me here, but you're right. We can't stay in the city. I'm going to try to get us to my parents' place in Tennessee."

"Mike, what about you?" Zeke questioned.

"I don't have anybody here. All of my family is

scattered around Oregon. I didn't think it was possible to get there, but if you are going to California, that's pretty close to Oregon. I'll come with you and maybe try to get to my family once we get to California," Mike answered.

"L.C., what are you going to do?"

"Well, I guess I'm in the same boat as everybody here except for John," L.C. started. "Since Carol died, I don't have anything holding me anywhere. I have some friends who live nearby, but like we already discussed, staying in the area isn't an option. If your offer is genuine and not just out of pity, I'll come with you. I'll have a better chance in a group than by myself."

"The offer is not out of pity. Your company increases our chance of getting there," Zeke acknowledged. Of all the people present, L.C. was the one Zeke had hoped would join him. He respected L.C. as a person, and Zeke knew he had the ability to take care of himself. The gun he carried in his holster was an added bonus for the group. He had retired from Atlanta PD with over thirty years on the job. His experience would definitely contribute to the group's chances of successfully arriving in California.

"What's your plan?" L.C. asked as they began gathering the food from the break room.

"I have three-quarters of a tank of gas. I don't know if we'll be able to drive all the way out of the city or not. If we can't, we'll have to walk and find another vehicle somewhere along the way."

"You're a pilot," Meagan said hopefully. "Maybe we can rent an airplane and fly."

"It would be a pretty short trip," Mike objected. "They said the President's no fly order is being enforced by the Air Force. Any plane in the air will be shot down without warning."

"If the sickness is as bad as they're saying, I doubt that order will be enforced for long. There won't be anybody left to fly the military planes and those who are left aren't going to care about a private plane. Right now it isn't an option, though," Zeke agreed as he pressed on a piece of tape sealing a cardboard box he had filled with an assortment of food from the break room. He handed the tape to John, who was carrying his own box to the vending machine in the corner of the room.

With a fire ax from the hall, John quickly knocked out the Plexiglas front and they began dividing the food between the two groups.

"Do you mind if I grab one of those?" Mike asked as John pulled the row of Snickers out of the metal coil that dispensed them.

"You can do what you want with your share, but if I were you, I would hold off and grab something from the café. The stuff up there will spoil pretty quickly when it's no longer refrigerated. The candy will last forever," John suggested as he pulled the last of the snacks from the machine.

"Good point," Mike ceded. "While you guys are working on this, I'm going to run up to the café and make a bunch of sandwiches for the road. You want to give me a hand, Meagan?"

Thirty minutes later, everything of foreseeable value for the trip had been gleaned from the building and was being loaded into Zeke's truck and John's car.

As Meagan stretched to lift a box over the side of the truck bed, Zeke noticed her attire for the first time. She was wearing a tight skirt that reached to her knees with slits running up a foot on either side. His eyes followed her legs down to two inch heels that supported what he guessed was a hundred and thirty five pounds.

"Meagan?" he asked. "You go to the gym after work, don't you?"

"Yeah. Why?" she asked, her voice full of uncertainty.

"Do you have a change of clothes with you for after your workout?"

"Yes," she answered suspiciously. "I have a pair of jeans. Why?"

"Because you aren't going to be able to run in heels and a tight skirt and there's a good chance running is going to be a big part of your immediate future. You might want to change into your jeans and workout shoes before we leave," Zeke suggested as he grabbed a pair of jeans and running shoes from the tool box in the bed of his truck and walked into the stairwell to change out of his slacks and patent leather loafers.

When Zeke returned to the garage, his truck had been moved. Mike had parked it beside Meagan's Accord. One end of a red hose was buried in the Honda's gas tank. The other end disappeared into Mike's mouth. He suddenly spewed a geyser of clear liquid from his mouth as he lowered the hose into a bucket. He coughed violently as he wiped his mouth on the sleeve of his coveralls. "Every time I do that, I swear I'll never siphon another ounce of gas," he added to the end of a string of colorful vulgarities. He suddenly stopped when he saw Meagan staring at him. "I apologize for my language," he said as he looked at her with embarrassment. At sixty-one years old, he had been raised in a society where women were still esteemed and were to be protected and respected. Although he felt no remorse for his use of vulgar language, he had been raised not to swear in the presence of a lady. For that, he felt guilt.

Meagan smiled as she climbed into the back seat of the truck. "Don't worry about it, Mike."

Chapter 14

After they topped off both vehicles' gas tanks, Zeke followed John's car as it made a right turn out of the parking garage. John took a quick left at the T intersection and Zeke turned right. As he passed, he looked at the building where he had worked for the last five years. L.C., who was sitting in the front seat, voiced the sentiment Zeke was feeling. "I'll probably never set foot in there again. It was a pretty good place to work." As he spoke, his voice was devoid of emotion, but if the three in the car could have seen his eyes, they would have seen the sadness his voice failed to convey.

The four rode in silence for block after block. Each seemed lost in silent thoughts too private to share. As they continued through the business district, buildings shrank to single story edifices fronted with brick and rock rather than mirrored glass.

The well-lit streets were devoid of traffic, either pedestrian or vehicular. As Zeke slowly rolled through a red light, a police car shot out of a driveway at the far end of the intersection. The blue lights illuminated as it turned left into the lane, coming nose to nose with Zeke's truck.

"You've got to be kidding," Zeke stammered. "With everything going on, he's going to stop me for rolling through a light?"

As Zeke leaned to the left to pull his wallet out of his back pocket, L.C. exclaimed, "Those aren't cops, Zeke! Get us out of here!" The cruiser's front doors flew open and Civic pulled out of a lot behind them and slammed up against the truck's rear bumper. As two men with baggy pants and wife beaters boiled out of the police cruiser, Zeke realized L.C. was right -- but it was too late. They were trapped between the two cars with no room to maneuver.

The driver walked toward the passenger side of the truck with a handgun in his right hand, hanging limply at his side. "What da ya'll got in there that I need?" he yelled angrily while raising his gun toward the truck. "Everybody out. Now!" His partner stayed in the V between the body of the cruiser and the open door. He leaned against the car with casual disinterest, his arm resting on the roof.

L.C. had pulled his nickel plated pistol from its holster. He pressed his gun and arm tightly against the door panel, hiding both from the approaching thug. Zeke bent down, reaching for the pistol he kept beneath the driver seat.

"Forget it," L.C. said calmly. "I'll shoot, you drive. Put it in four wheel and when I drop him, put it in reverse and push that rice burner behind us out of the way. Once you have room, get us out of here."

Zeke silently nodded in agreement as he pulled the gear shift on the floor into four high and reached for the gear shift on the steering column.

"Not yet," L.C. whispered as he rolled his window down. "The reverse lights will give you away. Wait until I shoot."

The unsuspecting hooligan casually strutted past the mirror, shoved the muzzle of his pistol inside the cab and screamed, "Get out!"

L.C. raised his left arm as fast as a rattlesnake and tightly wrapped his hand around the slide of the pistol and pushed it forward to the windshield pillar while simultaneously raising his right arm with his own pistol to the gangster's face. Both guns went off at the same time. The gangster's bullet exploded a spider web pattern across the passenger side of the windshield. L.C.'s bullet smashed into the thug's cranium, dropping him beside the truck in an unmoving pile of wasted life.

L.C. bellowed, "Now!" as Zeke was already pushing the shifter up two notches into reverse and smashing the gas pedal to the floor. Plastic crunched as the front of the entrapping car was shattered by the pickup's steel rear bumper. The motion was slow at first as the truck fought to overcome the friction between the road and the tires on the car. Once the small car began to inch rearward, giving way to the pickup's weight and horsepower, the coefficient of friction between the car and the road decreased making it easier to push. Both vehicles picked up speed. L.C. dropped the gangster's pistol, which he still held in his left hand, onto the dash and leaned out his window. He slowly and methodically fired at the delinquent beside the cruiser who had suddenly gained a keen interest in what was happening and hid behind the door like the coward that he was. The Civic pivoted around the rear bumper and slammed into the left side of the truck as Zeke braked and pulled the gear shift back into drive and once again smashed the gas pedal into the floor.

The engine roared as the truck surged forward and shot passed the hijacked police cruiser. L.C. fired one last round as the truck was even with the gangster, who was raising his gun in their direction. The shot flew true and the kid, who was in his early twenties, fell backward into the police cruiser. "Stop the truck!" L.C. yelled to be heard above Meagan's screams in the backseat. "The cruiser still has the rifle and shotgun in the gun rack."

Before the truck came to a stop, L.C. opened the door, jumped onto the asphalt road, and began to run the fifty feet back to the cruiser. Shots rang out from the red import. L.C. hunched down low as he ran and fired two shots. His gun went dry and he instinctively grabbed for the spare magazine in a pouch on his belt. Reaching the protection of the car door, he shoved the empty magazine into his pocket and put two more shots into the scraped driver's side of the Civic.

Then, as if he had lost interest in the bullets slamming into the cruiser's door, he reholstered his pistol and ducked into the car. Slivers of glass spewed into the interior as bullets pounded holes through the windshield. The interior began emitting a high pitched beep from the unlocked gun holder and L.C. emerged with an assault rifle in one hand and a shotgun in the other. Slinging the shotgun over his shoulder, he began walking backwards toward the pickup while firing into the Civic with the rifle.

Whether it was because the overwhelming firepower had forced the shooter to take cover or because one of the bullets had found a meaty target, the gunshots from the Civic ceased. L.C. slammed the truck door closed and shouted, "Make like a bread truck and haul buns!"

Chapter 15

This time Zeke didn't slow below forty for red lights. Two times in the next mile and a half, cars pulled out of lots and accelerated to follow. Both times Zeke romped on the gas and accelerated to seventy miles an hour. Both times, the cars immediately pulled back into parking lots without pursuit, waiting for easier targets.

Shortly after outrunning the last of the car pirates, the road began to plug up with abandoned cars. Initially Zeke was able to weave between the empty vehicles discarded in the lanes, but eventually the road was completely blocked. Driving on sidewalks and in parking lots took them a little further. When no more progress was possible, he turned down side streets. They proved to be no better.

It became apparent that continuing in the truck was not going to be practical. "It looks like this is the end of the line," L.C. commented dryly. "We're going to have to walk from here." Before he got out of the truck, he handed the pistol he had taken from the gangster to Mike and gave Zeke the shotgun. "If the two of you don't mind, I think I'm going to keep the rifle for myself," he said as he stepped out of the truck, rifle in hand.

"I'm okay with that," Mike said as he opened the back door and stepped out beside L.C., slipping his newly acquired weapon into his waist band. "You obviously know how to use it."

Zeke reached under the front seat and pulled out a black pistol in a holster and fastened it to his belt before shoving the two spare magazines into his left pocket. He racked a round into the chamber of the shotgun and topped the magazine tube off with a round from the shell carrier on the butt stock before slinging the weapon over his shoulder.

As Meagan got out of the car and surveyed the chaos of the blocked street and people walking around aimlessly, L.C. commented, "I bet you're glad you ditched your skirt and heels." She looked down at her jeans and running shoes and looked back up, silently nodding her agreement. She was still in a state of shock from the chaos and violence she had experienced since leaving the office.

"Zeke, is there any chance you have a backpack in your tool box?" L.C. questioned. "We're going to have a heck of a time carrying all this food the way it's boxed up."

Zeke unlocked the tool box and pulled a day pack out. "This is all I have," he answered as he dumped spare clothes out of the bag and into the tool box. "It will hold a little bit of the food."

"How about this?" Mike said, pulling a rolling suitcase out of a nearby abandoned car. Once the clothing was dumped into the backseat of the car the bag came from, the food was transferred into the case.

"Let's make some tracks," L.C. urged as he looked at the mob of people milling around without purpose. It was as if they had never considered how to travel without a vehicle.

"Hold on a second," Zeke said, pointing to a woman convulsing on the sidewalk. "She looks like the infected people they showed on the news." He cut a T-shirt from his back pack into four pieces and tied one piece around his face like a mask. "It can't hurt," he added, handing the pieces of white cloth to the other members of the group.

With cloth masks around their faces, the group started walking between the cars and people. Just ahead a woman started screaming while attempting to maintain control of a backpack a man was trying to wrest from her grasp. "That's all the food I have!" she pleaded.

"It's more than I have," he yelled angrily as he backhanded her. She lost her grip on the bag and fell to the ground, smashing the back of her head on the pavement.

The man stood over her as another woman ran and bent over to help her up. A moment later, the good Samaritan looked up and yelled, "She's dead! You killed her!"

"It didn't have to be this way," the man argued. "She should have just given me the bag. I didn't want to hurt her."

The woman kept yelling, "He killed her!"

Three kids in their late teens gathered around the man who was clutching the backpack in his hand. "Why don't you hand it over to us," the apparent leader of the group commanded as he bumped the man with his chest.

"But it's mine," the man protested.

"Actually, it was hers," the leader said, pointing to the woman lying on the ground, her hair matted with sticky blood. "Now we're going to take care of it," he proclaimed as he placed his hand on the bag and attempted to pull it away from the man. As the man tried to retain possession, another of the kids hit him in the side of the head. He stumbled under the ferocity of the blow and dropped to his knees. The leader kicked him in the gut. The man doubled over in pain and the trio brutally kicked him until he fell to the ground and lay motionless. The leader stood next to his head and raised his foot several feet off the ground and stomped down on the man's head. Unsatisfied with the results, he smirked and nonchalantly said, "I guess the human skull is stronger than I thought," as he lifted his foot again.

"That's enough!" Zeke thundered before the foot could crash down again. "Leave him alone."

"And who are you to tell me what I can and can't do?" the kid asked cockily as he started closing the distance between himself and Zeke.

"I'll tell you who I am," Zeke said as he unslung the shot gun and took a step forward to meet the approaching kid. "I'm the guy who's going to blow your head off your shoulders and paint your buddies' faces with your brains if you don't move on." L.C. took two steps and came even with Zeke, leveling his AR-15 at one of the other kids in a silent request that he not cause any more problems.

"All right," the kid said as he raised his hands even with his shoulders. "You're pretty brave when you've got that twelve gauge pointed at my head. Without that, you would be laying next to him," he tilted his head toward the unconscious man.

"Kid, you don't know the kind of pain you're about to bring down on yourself. I suggest you get out of here before he sets his gun down and pounds you into the pavement. Get going before I lose my patience and shoot you myself," L.C. said and advanced toward the three kids.

Sensing they were severely outmatched, they turned and strutted away with the bag of food.

After a mile or two, the number of cars thinned out to the point the road would have been drivable if they had a vehicle. The road was still littered with abandoned vehicles, many of which were left dead in the lane, presumably out of gas. Mike opened a door as they passed a late model sedan. He stuck his head in it for a second and said, "No keys," as he pulled back out. "These people aren't going back home and they aren't going to be driving their car anymore. Why do you suppose they took the keys with them?" he asked as he opened another door to look inside.

"It's habit," Meagan said, speaking for the first time in nearly an hour.

"I guess you're right," Mike answered, slamming another door shut.

"What difference does it make?" Meagan asked. "I mean, if the car worked, they wouldn't have left it here, right?"

Mike shook his head in disagreement, "These cars work fine. The only problem is they ran out of gas. We might be able to find some fuel around here somewhere. If we can find fuel, we can drive." As he opened the door of a black Volkswagen Jetta TDI, he was greeted with the ding ding ding he had been looking for. "Bingo!" he exclaimed as he pulled a single key from the ignition. He reinserted the key, twisted it forward, and waited as the gauges came to life. The gas gauge was pegged on empty.

"All right, we ought to be able to find some diesel around here," Mike said. "There should be a semi somewhere close by with all of these warehouses." The others looked around. They were in the middle of an industrial area of the city. After walking through lot after lot and climbing over one chain link fence after another, they found a warehouse with a semi truck backed up to a loading dock.

Mike climbed into the cab looking for keys. "Nothing!" he shouted down. "We need a bucket and a hose and we can siphon some fuel for the car."

L.C. disappeared around the corner of the building and returned a minute later. "Here's a hose," he said, carrying a big green coil of garden hose.

Zeke said, "I think there was a five-gallon bucket in the lot by the first building we looked at." He pulled himself up the fence which swayed back and forth under his weight. His shirt caught as he swung over the top and ripped the side. "Be right back," he shouted.

"Be careful," Meagan yelled after him as he jogged off into the darkness.

Zeke ran down the empty streets, backtracking to the first lot they had searched. As he neared the lot, he saw another person walking toward him. As the distance between them decreased, Zeke began to slow. Something wasn't right. The approaching figure was moving with a very awkward gait. It walked with stiff knees as it hobbled toward him.

"Are you okay?" Zeke hollered to the figure. It stopped moving and turned its head toward him as if it had just noticed him. The security lights on the sides of the buildings that flanked the road didn't provide adequate illumination in the street. He still couldn't make out any features of the individual. Zeke addressed the person again. This time, it responded with a howl that froze him in his tracks. It eyed him for a moment and charged as he unslung his shot gun.

Even with the awkward gait, it was fast. Zeke knew he only had moments to respond before it reached him. He was sure it was a sick person, but human life is sacred. He held his fire as the distance shrunk. The person's features clarified as it drew nearer. She was a teenage girl about seventeen years old. Her shoulder length, auburn hair fluttered behind her in the breeze created by her forward motion. And then he saw her face. It was twisted in a savage fury. Her lips were pulled back, showing two rows of straight teeth which were separated by the gap of her wide open mouth. Dark stains surrounded her mouth, running down her chin to her soiled shirt. She snarled and lunged toward him, her arms stretched out with grasping fingers, searching for a purchase on his body.

Realizing the mortal danger he was in, but still resisting the screaming urges from his mind to shoot her, he sidestepped to the left and stroked her head with the hard plastic butt of the Remington clenched in his hands.

The blow momentarily knocked her to her knees. Before he could regain his composure, she was back on her feet. Tilting her head back, she shrieked at the sky, and lunged at him a second time. Again, he sidestepped. He slammed the butt of the gun into the bridge of her nose as her head dropped toward his left arm which was entrapped within her iron grasp. Her head snapped back in response to the concussive impact, but she didn't release his arm.

He hit her again and again. Each blow visually devastated her face. Her nose was a flattened mess of skin and blood. Her left cheek bone was unnaturally caved into her face. The side of her head was saturated in blood from a split in her scalp. None of that seemed to have any effect on her actions and her grip on his arm remained as strong and unwavering as ever. Images he had seen on the television of people being eaten alive flashed through his mind. As he fought, he began to panic. He tried to point the barrel of the shot gun at her, but they were too close to each other.

Her other hand latched onto his arm like a vice and pulled it toward her cavernous mouth with unnatural strength. The Remington was now a hindrance. He released his grip on it and moved his hand to her throat as the gun clattered against the hard asphalt. He squeezed with all his strength, trying to strangle the life out of his assailant.

Her teeth snapped together just short of his arm. She snarled in frustration as he continued to keep his entangled arm mere inches from her mouth. Zeke kicked at her legs and drove his knee into her abdomen to no avail. As the battle raged on, his strength began to wane. She fought with unwavering strength and ferocity, even after he felt her trachea crush within his grasp. Nothing he did diminished her determination to consume his flesh. He realized the outcome of the battle was already settled. His resistance was simply delaying the inevitable. He refused to give in, yet he knew he could not win. She seemed to have a bottomless reservoir of power that he could not hope to match.

His muscles began to tremble with fatigue. His left arm pulled with as much force as he could muster while his right arm pushed her head away with an equal amount of force. In an act of final desperation, he stepped into her and placed his right leg half a step behind her. As he continued forward, her stinking breath blasted him in the face and the acrid stench brought an involuntary wretch from the pit of his stomach.

His right leg tripped her up and she stumbled backwards, pulling him down with her. Having anticipated the result of his action, he pushed away as far as he could and brought his knee up to his chest as he went down. She landed on her back and he landed on top of her, his knee crushing her sternum. With his knee keeping her at bay, he pulled his right arm from her throat and grasped for the pistol belted to his side. In a blinding flash, he pulled it free of the holster. He slammed the end of the barrel tight against the side of her head and jerked the trigger. The resulting explosion instantly ceased all signals from her warped brain and her body went limp beneath him.

His shoulders slumped and his chest heaved in and out, desperately drawing hot, humid air into his lungs. A minute later, after having regained his breath, Zeke stood on shaky legs and walked around the building where he had seen the bucket.

Chapter 16

With the orange five-gallon bucket in hand, Zeke returned to the group. "Are you okay?" L.C. questioned. "We heard a gunshot."

"Yeah, I'm okay." Zeke answered, his voice full of emotion as the memory of his fight replayed in his mind. "I ran into a sick girl and she attacked me."

"You killed her, didn't you?" Meagan asked accusingly.

"I didn't have a choice, Meagan," he replied defensively. "She would have killed me if I didn't." He looked from Mike to L.C., seeking some sort of affirmation that he had done the right thing. He knew he didn't have a choice, but he was riddled with guilt. It was gnawing at him accusingly, tearing at the fiber of his being. Whatever was said about them on TV, they still looked like people. The fact that she was a girl made it even worse. Zeke had been taught from the time he was a boy to respect and protect girls. In spite of that, he had just killed one. The fact that it had been in defense of his life did little to alleviate the remorse he felt.

"What happened?" L.C. inquired, sensing to some extent the anguish Zeke was experiencing.

Zeke related the story of seeing the person in the road and then the attack. As he told the story, details and images he hadn't previously been aware of flashed into his mind. With each new memory, waves of emotion washed over him. He began to doubt whether he had done the right thing. By the time he finished the story, he was fighting tears. He paused a moment as he considered his words. "Maybe there was another way. Maybe I could have done something else to stop her," he languished.

L.C. put his hand on Zeke's shoulder. "Zeke, you didn't have a choice. We both saw the same news clips and heard people tell the same stories on TV. These things aren't people anymore. The people died and the virus turned them into animals. You did everything you possibly could have done to spare its life. You waited so long before taking action that it almost killed you. You need to stop beating yourself up over what happened." Zeke nodded his head, acknowledging what L.C. was telling him.

"You're going to experience all kinds of emotions over this during the next few days, but you need to focus on the fact that you didn't have a choice. Never question that you did the right thing." L.C.'s voice faltered almost imperceptibly and he hesitated for several seconds. When he continued, his voice was steady again.

"I was involved in two shootings during my career. Both of them tore me apart. I second guessed myself just like you're doing. My second shooting was caught on a security camera. Even after watching the video hundreds of times and seeing there was no other option, I still wondered if I could have done something else. We weren't made to take lives. That's God's responsibility, but sometimes, for one reason or another, He gives that task to us. If things keep on like they're going right now, you're going to have to do it again and the next time, it might be a regular person and not one of those infected things. Just know that what you're feeling is not unusual and almost everybody who has taken another person's life has felt the same grief. The guilt will pass over time, but it's going to get worse before it gets better. Can you live with it?" he asked sincerely.

"I'm going to have to," Zeke said dryly, feeling foolish for the emotions he was exhibiting. It felt like weakness to let the others see him in this state, but there was nothing he could do about it.

Seeing that Mike had managed to siphon a full bucket of fuel from the truck's tank, L.C. asked, "You ready to move out?"

"Yeah," Zeke said. "Let's go."

Chapter 17

Without a funnel to channel the fuel directly into the filler spout, Mike spilled at least a third of the bucket down the side of the car. From the bottom of the rear fender, it dripped onto his shoes before forming rivulets that ran toward the curb.

"Do you want me to go refill the bucket?" Zeke offered as he warily watched groups of people stream passed them.

"No, man, if this works, and there's no reason it won't, we're going to drive this baby into the lot, park it next to the truck, and siphon directly into the tank."

Mike fished the key out of his pocket, hopped into the driver seat, and turned the engine over for ten seconds without it catching. "That's what I figured," he muttered just loud enough to be audible. "Zeke or L.C., one of you guys pull out the back seat. There's a fuel pump beneath it. You'll need to pull out the plastic trim around the two car seat latches and then you can lift the seat up. Pull up the carpet and take off the round cover in the middle to get at the pump. I'm going to work on accessing the pump in the engine compartment." Turning to Meagan, he asked, "Mind if I take that tool bag off your hands?"

She was quick to relinquish the small canvas bag she had been carrying since Mike had discovered it in the side compartment of the semi. It contained an assortment of basic tools ranging from pliers and screw drivers to hammers and vice grips. It even had a roll of duct tape and a coiled section of rusty bailing wire. L.C. had joked that the owner of the truck must have been a farmer when he wasn't driving.

"Is there anything I can do to help?" L.C inquired.

"You a gear head?" Mike asked.

"No, short of changing the oil, I don't know how to do much, but if you point me in the right direction I'll do what I can."

"Alright," Mike said. "Use these pliers and loosen the two fittings here and here," he said as he tapped them with the pliers. "They're the injectors. We need to bleed the air out of the system. If it still won't run, we'll need to bust those two fittings loose over there, too, but I think these will be enough to get her running again."

Using a short piece of the bailing wire, Mike jumped the terminals on the fuel pumps, both of which hummed to life. Seconds later, fuel began spurting from the base of the loosened connections on the injectors. When he was satisfied with his work, he reattached the electrical connectors to the pumps, tightened the injector fittings, and got back in the car. "Cross your fingers," he said and turned the key. The engine turned over for several seconds with no effect before it began to sputter, and then suddenly roared to life. "Wachaaa!" Mike yelled in glee. "We're done walking!"

It only took a couple minutes to drive to the lot where the big rig was parked. Zeke, who was riding in the front passenger seat, slipped out of the car, put a bullet through the lock, and rolled the gate open enough to allow passage of the car. L.C pulled the car around the building and stopped beside the big rig.

Mike quickly had the siphon going again and stood by the fuel filler spout until diesel began overflowing. He quickly pulled the hose out, coiled it up, and yelled, "Hey, L.C., pop the trunk so I can stow this hose in case we need to refill down the road." There was a click and the trunk lid rose half an inch. Mike tossed the hose in next to the bucket and slammed the lid.

As soon as the lid shut, the locking mechanism clicked again and the lid rose half an inch. L.C. said, "Put your boots in there or you're walking. We're not going to smell that diesel stench all the way to California."

Chapter 18

An hour later, L.C. was driving west on a two lane highway away from Atlanta. There had been significant debate as to how to get to California. Mike had pushed for taking the northern route, picking up I-80, while L.C. wanted to take the southern route through Texas. Meagan and Zeke didn't have a preference.

In the end, L.C. won out by practicality. When they left Atlanta, the path of least resistance had taken them southwest of the city and they ended up on Highway 166 which more or less paralleled I-20. Highway 166 was a two lane highway, but at three in the morning, the traffic was manageable. Defunct vehicles had, for the most part, made their way onto the shoulder. Eventually, they planned to shoot up north to I-20, well west of Atlanta where they hoped traffic on the interstate would be lighter.

Everything went fine until they worked their way up to I-20 after thirty minutes of traveling on Highway 166. Even though they were thirteen miles from the city, traffic on I-20 was still snarled, crawling at a nearly imperceptible rate. They could hear horns blaring long before they saw the gridlock.

"This isn't going to work," Mike complained. "We should have taken the northern route."

"Maybe," Zeke said, "but do you think traffic would be

any better? I'm pretty sure every major freeway out of the city is going to look like this." Unfamiliar with the Jetta's GPS, Zeke's fingers fumbled as he searched for an alternate route. Scrolling through options, he found one that routed without traversing the Interstate freeway system. It was an option, he mused, that probably never got used. After about a minute, the computer spit out a new route to California. This scenic route was made up entirely of back roads.

"New plan," he said to L.C. "Turn this buggy around and head back to 166. We'll follow it through Carrollton and on into Alabama."

"Ten-four. Changing course. I'm going to need a break here before too long. Is anybody else up to driving for a while?" L.C. questioned through a sleepy yawn.

"I'm wide awake," Meagan offered. "Let me drive."

"Little lady, you don't have to offer twice," L.C. replied as he drifted out of the lane and onto the shoulder. "If you would be kind enough to swap places with me, I'm going to check out the back of my eyelids for a while." Within a couple minutes of having completed the switch, L.C. was snoring softly.

"Wake me up if you get tired or have any problems." Zeke said as he curled up against the door and closed his eyes. "Stay on this road until you reach Alabama."

An hour later, Zeke was awakened by a deep boom coupled with Meagan slamming on the brakes and screaming, "What do we do now?"

Zeke sat upright, his mind foggy as he was roused from deep sleep. His bearings returned quickly. They were at a complete stop in the road. On the shoulder just ahead of them was a digital traffic sign with a lighted message stating

"Closure enforced with deadly force." A hundred yards past the sign, the road was blocked with a concrete barricade, and a hundred feet beyond the barricade was the fiery hulk of a vehicle. The dancing flames illuminated a trail of grey smoke descending sharply from the sky to the car. The edges of the smoke trail still swirled angrily.

"What happened?" L.C. yelled from the backseat.

"The car I was following went around the barricade. I was about to follow it when a ball of fire appeared in the sky above the gas station over there. It raced down and the car exploded."

Zeke opened his door and jumped out of the car. The thumping of helicopter rotors eclipsed the roar of the lusty flames licking skyward from the shattered body of the unrecognizable vehicle ahead of them. Although he couldn't see the helicopter, he was able to discern that it was orbiting around them overhead. He looked from the burning vehicle to the advisory sign and back to the smoke trail that dissipated into the inky blackness of the night sky. The fire lit up enough of a smoke trail to extrapolate its trajectory to above the gas station where Meagan claimed the fireball had originated.

L.C., who had also exited the car, came to the same conclusion as Zeke and hastily crammed his six foot four inch frame back into the vehicle while yelling, "Get us out of here!"

Meagan was frozen in her seat, eyes glued to the inferno lighting up the road ahead. Terror grasped her body like a straightjacket, locking her in indecision. She knew she had to drive, but her body wouldn't respond to her wishes. She was aware of Zeke sliding back into the seat beside her and putting his left foot over the center console as his hand reached for the gear shift. He moved his hand to the steering wheel as he kicked her foot off the brake pedal. The engine screamed and the car ripped backwards as if it were about to be crushed by a demon escaping the fires of hell.

In the backseat, Mike was screaming, "Go! Go! Go!" Zeke needed no prodding. It only took an instant to realize that the road closure was being enforced by a military helicopter, probably from the Alabama National Guard. They were obviously serious about maintaining the sovereignty of their state line. As Meagan came out of her catatonia, she involuntarily lurched, hitting Zeke's arm. The impact was negligible, but at forty-five miles per hour, in reverse, it only took a small deviation of steering input to shoot the car off the road, through a fence and into a pasture. Pushing the brake pedal did little to slow the car on the dew soaked grass. The car continued to slide until it slammed into a tree.

Zeke, who was sitting astride the center console, was catapulted into the backseat where his body wedged between L.C. and Mike.

Chapter 19

Everybody sat stunned, dismayed by the carnage they had narrowly escaped. They all realized that if they hadn't been following another car, they would have driven passed the barrier and been blown to bits. The violence of the impact with the tree had shocked them into an unmoving silence. Zeke was unsure of how long he sat between L.C. and Mike before L.C. finally broke the silence.

"Is everybody okay?" he questioned.

"Just a little shaken," Mike answered.

"I'm all right," Meagan said slowly, realizing that she was responsible for the wreck.

"How about you, Zeke?" L.C. prodded. "Anything broken?"

"I don't think so, but everything hurts," Zeke stammered, still dazed from being slammed into the back seat.

"If they were going to blow us up, I think they already would have," L.C. quipped. "But, I would sure feel better if we didn't sit around and find out."

The car refused to budge no matter how much Meagan tried to coax it. Mike finally gave up hope and relented, "It looks like we're back to hoofing it, at least for the time being."

The quartet exited the car and was attempting to rub the

soreness out of their necks as they looked at the diminishing flames four hundred yards away.

Suddenly, a blinding spotlight illuminated behind them. "Are you all right?" a voice asked with genuine concern. As the group turned, they were blinded by an intense beam shining from the porch of a house fifty yards away.

L.C. answered for the group, "I think we're going to make it. We had a little accident. The helicopter just launched a missile at that car that's burning beyond the blockade. We were trying to get away before we became the next target. We're really sorry about your fence."

"Don't worry about the fence, Son," the voice said without malice. "That's the third car they've blown up tonight. The others made it a little further passed the roadblock. They're working extra hard to keep the infection from spreading into Alabama. The news says there aren't any confirmed cases there yet. Where are you folks heading?" the voice asked.

"We're on our way to California," Zeke answered, his hand shielding his eyes, trying see who was behind the light.

"Do you have a place to stay the night?"

"We were planning on driving straight through," Zeke answered as he stepped toward the voice on the porch.

"Hold it there, Son. I don't want you coming any closer. I'm going to get some blankets and set them on the porch. Ya'll can spend the night there. If ya'll are healthy in the morning, we'll be happy to feed you breakfast before you head out."

The light was extinguished and a spring squeaked as it pulled the screen door closed with a bang. Interior lights illuminated and a minute later, the porch light came on and the spring squeaked again as the screen was opened. An old man between eighty and ninety years old dropped a pile of blankets on the porch. A woman, five or ten years his junior, set a plate of something down on a patio table.

The old man spoke again. "The name's Lester and this is my lovely bride Mildred. I feel bad making you sleep outside, but until we're sure you not sick, we can't let you in. I hope you understand," he added apologetically. "Sleep tight. We'll see you in the morning."

"We understand and we're grateful for the hospitality," Zeke answered appreciatively.

"In case you're hungry, I set a plate of cookies on the table," the old woman said as an afterthought before she followed Lester through the doorway and back into the house. The screen slammed shut behind her. "I don't know about you guys, but I'm going to dig into those cookies," Mike exclaimed, bounding up the steps to the porch two at a time.

Zeke's watch showed 6:40 when the sun finally peaked up over the treetops behind the house, tossing a warm array of pink and orange along the base of the clouds scattered above the eastern horizon. Everyone else was still sprawled out on the porch. Mike and L.C. had laid their blankets on the redwood boards as a type of makeshift mattress. Meagan had chosen to curl up directly on top of the wooden planks and was using her blanket to chase off the chill of the cool morning air. Zeke had lost his desire to sleep and cautiously sat guard in an old lawn chair with faded nylon weave that threatened to finish unraveling and dump him on the ground if he moved the wrong way. His sore back and neck wouldn't allow him to sleep on the ground. Between the vehicle ahead of them being blown to smithereens and the crash, too much adrenaline had been dumped into his blood stream for him to sleep anyway.

As he pondered how to best continue the trip westward, he heard a lock click and the screen door spring squeak again. Lester emerged from the house looking none the worse for the late night visitors. Mike sat upright and stretched, attempting to work the stiffness out of his muscles. Meagan moaned lightly as a yawn escaped her lips. L.C. looked up at Lester, but other than a tilt of his head, didn't move.

"How's everybody feeling?" Lester asked, looking from person to person, inspecting each for signs of sickness. "If you had it, I suppose you would have symptoms by now, wouldn't you?" he asked thoughtfully. "You're probably hungry, aren't you? Why don't ya'll come on inside. Mildred baked up a pan of biscuits and made some gravy to go with them."

As the group moved inside, Zeke looked skyward at the helicopter which was still patrolling nearly a mile away. The original helicopter must have been spelled by another craft at some point during the night.

Following breakfast, Mildred stood up to clear the table. "I've got it," Meagan said as she put a hand on Mildred's shoulder and told her to sit back down. "You got up early to cook breakfast. I'll clean up the mess."

"I'll give her a hand," Mike volunteered. "You stay here and relax."

Several hours after breakfast, the six adults were sitting in front of the television, transfixed just as they had been the day before. Today, the video showed local carnage. The infection had taken hold in Atlanta and had spread to surrounding areas. As the infection spread, the infected began bunching up in groups. When they moved in ones and twos, they were easy to dispatch. As the groups grew, defenses were overcome by their sheer numbers. Videos showed larger and larger groups moving together. There was no discernible reason for where they went. Some groups stayed in urban areas where there were large numbers of people to prey upon. In other places groups traveled through the woods away from the city. The movement seemed to be random, according those who claimed to be experts on the day old phenomenon.

When coverage returned to national news, the local station occasionally interrupted the network feed to advise of the location of a large horde moving through an area. At about 2:30 in the afternoon, the local anchor came on screen to report that a horde of at least a hundred infected was moving west out of Bowden along Highway 166.

"We're on Highway 166 right now," Meagan stammered with terror edging through her voice. "How far is Bowden from here?" she asked in a wavering voice.

"It's less than three miles, sweetie," Mildred answered, not picking up on the reason for Meagan's fear.

L.C. briskly rose from his seat and strode to the door. "Come on, Zeke. I have a bad feeling we're about to need those long guns that are out in the car."

Part 3

Lost Hills, California
Friday Morning

Chapter 20

Connor slept fitfully. All night he tossed and turned, unable to get comfortable. No matter how he lay, an injured portion of his body was bearing his weight. During the brief moments he was able to contort his body to avoid putting pressure on broken ribs or bruised organs, his head ached so badly that he couldn't settle into the repose he sought. As dawn approached, he finally drifted off into a reprieve from his pain.

The sound of a gunshot brutally pulled Connor from his slumber. Rays from the morning sun poured into the room through the windows, illuminating it with a soft light as he opened his eyes. Connor looked around in confusion, trying to remember where he was and why his body hurt. Images from the previous days flooded through his memory. Additional gunshots drove daggers into his throbbing head as he swung his feet to the floor and searched the room for his pants.

He saw them folded in a chair in the corner, his duty belt coiled on top. Gunshots continued to sporadically *pop*. He pulled the curtain back, trying to glimpse the action, but the gunfire was on the other side of the house. In a rush to join the fracas, he buckled his gun belt around his waist and ran out of the room wearing nothing but his white briefs and gun belt, his pants still folded neatly on the chair.

His body brutally punished him with every stride as he

dashed through the open front door and sprinted down the wraparound porch. A rifle boomed again. As he rounded the corner, gun in hand, he stopped and stared in dismay. He tried to scurry back around the corner before he was seen, but it was too late.

"I think you forgot your pants, Connor. How hard did Curtis hit you last night?" Matt asked, doubling over in laughter as Toby leaned his rifle against the rail and Luke removed his earmuffs. The boys looked wide-eyed at Connor as he stood before them in a pair of sparkling white briefs. "With all the shooting you've done in the last couple days, I wouldn't have figured you needed any range time," Matt added, wiping tears from his eyes.

"What's all the laughing about?" Katie's voice burst out from around the far corner of the house. She followed Eve as the two walked into view. Both stopped short, seeing Connor standing dumbfounded and embarrassed. Katie put her hand to her mouth as she tried to hide the smirk that threatened to explode into laughter. She quickly crossed the distance between herself and her husband.

"I thought they were shooting at infected..." he trailed off, realizing there was nothing he could say that was going to make the situation any better.

Katie gently wrapped her arm around his waist and turned him back to the front door. As they walked up the stairs, Katie managed to stifle her laughter, but couldn't wipe the grin from her face.

"Pretty stinking funny, isn't it?" Connor asked, obviously still smarting from embarrassment. "A guy tries to protect his family and this is what he gets."

"Come on, Connor. If you could have seen yourself standing on the porch in your tighty whities with your gun strapped to your hip, you would be laughing, too." She lifted his folded pants from the chair as they walked into the room and handed them to him. "How are you feeling?"

"I feel like I was run over by one of those pavement grinders and then somebody else drove over me with a steam roller," he said while gingerly rubbing a broken rib. As he bent over to pull his pants on, he groaned in discomfort.

"Why don't you finish getting dressed," she said, running her fingers through his hair, "and I'll fix you some breakfast."

After painfully getting into his clothes, Connor limped down the stairs. When he entered the kitchen, Merv and Frank, with steaming cups of coffee in front of them, were sitting at the table talking to Zack.

Zack looked up as Connor entered the room. In spite of everything that had happened, he was still wearing his jovial smile. "Well, look at you," he quipped. "It looks like you got run over by a herd of elephants. At least you had the decency to put some pants on before making your grand appearance in the kitchen."

Connor shot a dirty look at Katie who sheepishly raised her gaze from the pan of eggs she was scrambling at the stove. She shrugged her shoulders innocently, trying to give the impression she wasn't the one who ratted him out.

"Don't worry about it," Zack said lightheartedly. "Sometimes I dream that I'm back in high school and I when look down, I realize I'm naked. I know exactly how it feels to have everybody looking at you, thinking you've lost it. Now that I think about it, though, my experience with walking around naked is limited to the realm of dreams. Maybe doing it in real life is a sign that you really have lost it."

Turning from Connor to Frank, Zack asked, "What do you think Frank? Has Connor lost it?"

Frank, who was still reeling from the loss of his brother, wasn't ready to join Zack in needling Connor. He self-consciously stood up from the table and, with a weak smile, said, "I think I need to go change the oil in my ATV or something," and quickly walked out of the kitchen.

Matt entered the room as Frank was walking out. Looking around, he sensed he had walked in on the tail end of an awkward situation. Unsure of what he had stumbled upon and not wanting to sit in the uncomfortable silence that was palpably clinging to the room, he stated his business. "I've been calling Wim Cummings all morning to see if he's going to finish drilling the well at the high school today. He hasn't answered any of my calls, so I'm heading into town to check the well site and see if he started working. I can't imagine he'd start without us being there to provide cover for them after yesterday's attack, but who knows."

"I'll come with you," Zack said, eager to escape the tension he had created with his joking around.

"Me, too," Connor said.

"No," Matt objected, shaking his head. "You're going to stay here and recuperate. Right now, you would be more of a hindrance than a help. If we're faced with a mob of infected like we were yesterday, we may have to run and you're in no shape for that."

Connor started to argue, but he knew Matt was right. He was still suffering from a concussion and his whole body ached. As much as he wanted to go and help, he knew he wasn't fit to fight in his current condition.

"Go get Frank," Merv said. "He and I both need something to get our minds off Jeb. I'll go get my rifle and meet you out front in a minute."

Ten minutes later, the four heavily armed men were making their way back into Lost Hills in a Hummer. The vehicle looked like a porcupine with rifles barrels bristling out all four windows.

Merv had flatly rejected the AR-15 Matt offered him before they left. He said he wouldn't go into battle with a plastic gun. Instead, he took his bolt action Winchester .270 and a Ruger .44 magnum pistol.

The county roads into town were completely deserted. They passed a caravan of two heavily loaded cars on the outskirts of town. The driver of the lead car offered a rigid wave of greeting. Matt slowed the Hummer and both approaching cars slowed in response.

Matt's window was down, his rifle barrel sticking out, ready for whatever threat may appear. He pointed the rifle up as the car drew alongside the stopped Hummer.

"Are you going to turn us back?" the driver asked, his nervousness apparent by the shaky timber of his voice.

"No. Far be it from me to tell a man how to take care of his family," Matt said, looking at two scared young faces peering out from around a pile of stuff crammed into the back seat. He doubted they would be able to get out of the car without the cargo being unloaded first. "Where are you headed?" he asked with genuine interest.

"We're going to Idaho," came the brief reply.

Realizing no more conversation was forthcoming, Matt nodded, wished him good luck, and resumed the trek to the well site.

Four blocks from the school, Zack, who was sitting in

the front seat, told Matt to stop. Before he had a chance to explain, Merv loosed a thundering shot from his rifle. A high pitched ringing erupted in Zack's ears in response to the gunshot. One of the three infected standing two hundred yards out slumped to the ground as if somebody had turned its power switch off. Two seconds later, Merv eased the trigger rearward sending another bullet hurtling down the twenty six inch steel barrel. A second infected was knocked head over heels, landing beside the first. Without taking his eye away from the scope, he worked the bolt in a smooth, rapid motion. In a continuous movement, his hand moved from the bolt to the trigger where he fired his third shot. The last infected, now running toward them, stumbled and fell to the ground, legs still twitching in response to expected signals that were no longer being transmitted to the large muscles.

The clash had lasted five seconds from start to finish. Even Zack grinned in approval and admiration at Merv's shooting exhibition. Like a professional, Merv calmly placed three more rounds in the rifle.

Zack took his calmness as a sign he had previously been in combat. "This isn't your first rodeo, is it?" Zack asked.

"No," Merv answered without emotion. "I did a tour in Vietnam at the start of the war."

"I guess that explains why you didn't want to take a plastic gun into battle."

"I've used 'em a little and I didn't much care for 'em. Back in 'Nam, I mostly carried a .300 Winchester."

"The way you shoot the rifle you're carrying, I don't figure there's any need to try to talk you into trying the semi auto with a larger magazine capacity," Zack ceded. "That was an impressive display of marksmanship."

Merv silently acknowledged the compliment with a slight nod of his head as Matt resumed driving.

Chapter 21

Four blocks later, the Hummer pulled to a stop at the baseball field. All four doors swung open in unison as if it had been a practiced event. The men exited the vehicle and approached the drilling rig. Everything was as it had been the previous day, with no signs that any additional work had been performed since the attack.

The mass of dead infected bodies surrounding the flatbed truck was untouched. A buzz filled the air as flies moved from one corpse to the next. Matt was thankful his gas mask cut out the noxious smell of death he knew had settled into the area and was increasing as the bodies decomposed under the heat of the midmorning sun.

Frank stared with empty eyes as the events that led to his brother's infection replayed in his memory. In his mind, he saw an infected man bound up the backside of the flatbed, drag his brother off the other side, and then struggle with him on the ground. He saw Jeb's gas mask knocked askew in the fight and then saw it fall to the ground as Frank rushed to his brother's aid, shooting the attacking beast. He hadn't had time to dwell on the horror of seeing Jeb lying face down on a dead, bloody body without the protection of his gas mask because more infected had boiled around both ends of the truck and he had been forced to engage the onslaught as it threatened to sweep over them. He recalled the sound of Jeb's rifle pounding away at infected coming around the front of the truck even as he was engaging those coming around the back end. He had looked over his shoulder to check on Jeb when he had a brief respite in the attack. Jeb was smashing the butt of his rifle into the bridge of an infected's nose as he ejected an empty magazine and slammed a fresh one into his rifle and resumed his barrage of fire.

Frank had turned back to resume his own desperate battle, trusting his brother to protect his back. He remembered the relief when the rush ended and he saw Jeb was still standing. The relief was short lived. It had only taken a second to realize Jeb's face was covered in blood and gore. His gas mask was buried somewhere deep in the pile of bodies at his feet.

There was no possible way he could have avoided exposure to the virus. The probability that he was immune to the disease was so slight that it wasn't worth mentioning, yet he had clung to it. Hours later, his fears had been confirmed when Matt, Connor, and Zack had pulled up to the Black family home without Jeb.

As Frank thought back over the past eighteen hours, the emotion returned with its raw biting pain. His vision clouded as tears began to accumulate in his eyes. He slung his rifle over his shoulder and walked back to the Hummer several steps ahead of the others.

As the Hummer pulled to a stop in front of the Cummings' home, fears of Cummings' demise were reinforced by the broken windows in the front of the house. The siding beneath two broken out windows had been stained by blood which had dried to a dark red, bordering on brown. Several dead infected lay below the windows. Homes up and down the street bore similar damage.

They had seen the same thing the afternoon before, prior to the attack on the well drilling crew. Infected trapped within their homes had escaped by breaking through windows.

The foursome approached the broken out window at the front of the house, rifles raised, safeties off, and ready for action. Matt yelled, "Anybody home?" as his boot ground a petunia into the soft dirt of the flower bed. He didn't expect an answer. He yelled because he knew any infected inside the house would more than likely be drawn to the sound of his muffled voice. He waited patiently. Getting no response, he yelled again. Still with no response, he was finally convinced the house was empty.

"Hold up," Zack said, stopping Matt just before he climbed over the casement into the living room. "Look at that," he said, pointing at the ground beneath the window. "There isn't a single piece of glass outside. It's all on the inside. This window was broken from the outside, not the inside."

Frank, who had taken a position to cover the other broken window when Matt yelled into the house, spoke up. "This one was broken from the outside, too."

Matt raked the butt of his rifle across the bottom of the window frame, knocking loose shards of glass free before climbing into the living room. The others followed, guns in the ready position as they entered the interior of the house. The living room had been ransacked. The wall opposite the end of the hallway had taken an apparent shotgun blast. A three inch hole had been blown out of the sheet rock. Moving outward from the center hole, dozens of small holes dotted the wall, decreasing in number and density further out. Two infected lay side by side in a pool of sticky, half coagulated blood.

As they started down the hall, Merv slung his deer rifle over his shoulder and drew his pistol from its holster as he stepped over two more infected that lay in the hallway, their faces unrecognizable as a result of close range shotgun blasts. At the end of the hall, Matt and Zack burst around the corner into the master bedroom.

It was obvious from the carnage in the room that Wim had put up a vicious fight. Pictures and broken frames lay on the floor, keepsakes had been strewn from the dresser top, and the bodies of seven infected lay around the room. As valiant as his fight had been, though, Wim had come up short in the end. He, and what Matt assumed were the remains of his wife, lay in the corner of the room. There wasn't much left of either of them.

Stricken with grief, Matt punched the wall, caving in a hole beneath his fist. Without another word, the group walked out of the room, down the hall, and out the front door.

Nobody spoke as they returned to the farm. There was nothing to say. The infected had ratcheted up their aggression. Previously they had been content to prey on those in the open. Now, they appeared to be forcing their way into homes to slaughter those taking refuge within. Virtually every house they passed showed signs of infected either breaking out of the home or into it.

Each time they saw infected, they stopped and killed them. Several died in futile attempts to attack the vehicle. Others fell under the long range assault of Merv's rifle. They estimated his farthest shot at nearly five hundred yards.

As they drove through town, they spotted a handful of people coming out of stores. They were well armed, but were still moving with a haste borne of fear. They weren't looting so much as they were procuring the necessities for survival, and nobody faulted them for leaving the store with carts full of food.

"What do we do now?" Frank asked dejectedly.

"We band together and fortify for a fight," Merv answered, his voice full of determination and resolve. "We aren't going to end up like the rest of those people."

Part 4

Bowden, Georgia
Friday Morning

Chapter 22

The "Bowden Horde," as it was being called, was the largest one seen to date according to the commentator. A news helicopter followed it to a quarter mile from the Alabama line. The mass of bodies ambled along following the road. From the sky, it resembled an amoeba with fingers surging ahead or to the side only to be reabsorbed by the main body.

The onward march halted briefly when a finger branched out to the edge of the road and pushed against a fence holding a lone cow. The sheer weight of the group was sufficient to splinter the boards. The cow started to run, but the movement drew the horde's attention. Initially three individuals broke into a sprint after it and then more joined the pursuit. The cow didn't have anywhere to go in the small field. Twenty bodies promptly covered it like ants on a candy bar. The growing swarm took it to the ground, where it kicked briefly before being subdued by the hungry onslaught. Death quickly followed. A man came out of a house a short distance away and raised a gun to his shoulder. In an instant, the mob's attention was diverted toward the farmer. Forgetting the cow, the group moved in unison toward the rancher, who quickly retreated into the security of the home. The helicopter descended low enough that the camera could frame the front door.

As with the wooden fence, the force of the bodies

pushing against it forced the door open. The farmer was briefly glimpsed in the high power lens, gun to his shoulder, standing firm, before he was overcome and disappeared into the mass of nearly twenty bodies. The anchor woman announced that the helicopter was dangerously low on fuel and had to return to the airport. Prior to turning back, the camera zoomed out to give a wide angle view of what was happening. The horde was continuing its march down the highway, minus fifteen or twenty individuals that had come out of the house and returned to the bloody cow carcass.

"That was Kenny Smith," Lester commented somberly in disbelief. "They just killed Kenny."

Everybody moved to the east side of the house where they could look out the large picture window. The advancing group was visible a quarter mile down the road, ambling toward them as if taking a relaxing jaunt. Six minutes later, it was nearly even with the house, but still in the road.

Mildred, who had been sitting, suddenly stood, lines of panic chiseled in her ashen face. "Where's Templeton?" she asked, hobbling across the room. "Templeton!" she yelled. "Where are you, Templeton?"

In response, there was a high pitched, whiny bark from the front porch. If the bark wasn't enough, the shrill squeak of the spring when Mildred opened the screen, followed by the loud bang of it slamming into its frame behind the miniature dachshund, turned every head on the road. The throng howled in unison as it charged the house.

The house sat on a basement constructed of cinderblock walls. Only four feet of it was actually below ground level. The top half of the basement was above the ground but had no windows. It looked like a tall foundation. The extra five feet put the windows of the first story above the reach of the infected. The only entrance into the house was up the porch and through the front door.

Zeke and L.C. took up positions side by side at the far end of the living room, across from the front door. L.C calmly lifted his rifle to his shoulder and looked from Zeke to Mike before focusing on the door. "Fellows, better make every shot count," he admonished as he snapped the safety off and moved his finger from the frame of the rifle to the trigger and awaited his first target.

Tracking the advance of the infected didn't require looking out the window. In fact, everybody had moved away from the windows, hoping that remaining out of sight would also keep them out of the half-witted minds outside the house. The sonorous shrieks provided all the information needed to determine the location of the swarm. Meagan jumped and yelped when a running body thudded into the side of the house hard enough to rattle a window and knock a picture off the wall. The frame crashed down, sending shards of glass skittering across the hardwood floor. Feet pounded hollowly on the steps to the porch. Footfalls softly tread up and down the length of the porch. Heavy breathing replaced the guttural howling, keeping pace with the sounds of walking feet.

Then the clamor ceased. Silence hovered over the house like a morning mist clinging to the ground. Nobody moved, inside or out. The moment of truth had arrived. Had the group lost interest in a meal it had not seen and was preparing to move on, or was it simply perplexed by the puzzle of the closed door?

Zeke unconsciously held his breath, not daring to hope that they would simply lose interest. It was too much to ask for, and he knew without a doubt what the result would be if they breached the house. Kenny Smith's demise, broadcast to the world, removed any question of that. The infected would swarm the six individuals in the house like Alaskan mosquitoes on a fly fisherman standing in the shade. They would be torn apart, screaming in agony as they were slowly devoured alive, one bite at a time.

Zeke released his breath as the first body hit the screen door. The force of the impact caused the door to rebound off the frame just far enough for the spring to pull it closed again with a resonant bang. The sound was all that was needed to recapture the attention of the entire mass of rotting flesh. Feral voices wailed and bayed against the entrance. Thumps and thuds throbbed relentlessly against the door. Each resounding bang of the screen fueled the fire of madness building outside. The fervor of the throng reached a crescendo as the wooden frame of the screen snapped audibly.

"Get the women upstairs!" L.C. barked to Lester. "Get behind a locked door and barricade it with whatever you can."

Templeton whimpered pathetically from behind the chair when Mildred got up. She stumbled in terror as she moved toward the stairway. To her credit, Meagan maintained her composure and grabbed Mildred's arm, keeping her from falling to the floor. Lester took the lead as they made their way up the flight of oak steps.

Zeke suddenly leaned his shotgun against the wall and ran across the room toward the door.

"What are you doing? Get back here!" L.C. shouted after him.

"I'm going to try to brace the door," Zeke said as he

grabbed onto the edge of the heavy oak table and began dragging it toward the front door. Once he reached the entrance, Zeke upended the table and shoved it against the door. As he crossed the room to move more furniture, an increasingly loud *thump thump thump* began to eclipse the cacophony of noises from the ravenous beasts outside.

"It's the military helicopter," L.C. yelled. Confirming his statement, a deep, continuous booming accompanied chunks of the road flying into the air as the twenty millimeter canon tore through the press of bodies scrambling toward the house. The massive projectiles ripped through flesh and bone and slammed into the roadway. The armor piercing rounds were designed to smash through tank armor and the road was much softer than hardened tank steel. The high velocity rounds plowed a bloody furrow down the middle of the road, splaying bodies into pieces.

The infected continued their assault, undeterred and oblivious to the death raining down on them from above. If anything, the noise fanned them into an even greater frenzy than before. Zeke watched through a window as the massacre unfolded. The helicopter entered a side-slipping circular path that kept the nose and canon pointed toward the rapidly advancing center of the group. As the torrent of bullets ripped into the middle of the crowd, bodies fell to the ground and were churned into a bloody conglomeration of flesh and dirt.

Within seconds, the throng of bodies around the house had been reduced to a handful of crawlers and stragglers. All that was left of the original mob were the thirty or forty that had already made it onto the porch and were still slamming against the door, attempting to gain entrance to the house.

Zeke watched the helicopter side slip until it was facing the front of the house twenty feet off the ground and four hundred yards away. In a heart stopping moment, he realized what was about to happen. "Take cover!" he screamed as puffs of smoke erupted from the nose of the helicopter and were driven to the ground and rolled to the sides, driven by the force of the rotor wash.

The helicopter instantly converted the house to a gazebo as bullets blasted through the front and back walls. The door was blown to bits and infected that hadn't been pulverized by the salvo boiled into the living room, chased by more rounds from the cannon. Staying was not an option. If the infected didn't rip him to shreds, the helicopter would. "We've got to get out of here!" he screamed over his shoulder to L.C. and Mike.

It was too late. Mike and L.C. were down. A round from the helicopter had more or less cut Mike in two. He was dead before his body hit the ground. L.C. was on his back, drenched in blood. Zeke couldn't tell if he was hit by a bullet or flying debris. The infected poured into the room, their focus locking onto the two men straight ahead. Unaware of Zeke's presence in the corner of the room, they ignored him. As they darted past he fired his pistol, but to no avail. There were too many and they were moving too fast. Seven or eight of them dropped on Mike and L.C. in a feeding frenzy, their disgusting shrieks and howls failing to cover L.C.'s agonizing cries for help. Another five or six were drawn to the stair case by the uncontrolled, panicked wails from upstairs, and more continued to pour through the door.

Zeke started for L.C., but he knew it was too late. Even

if he could get the pack away from him, they had already ripped into him. He was exposed and would become infected if he survived the assault.

With no way to help the others in the house, Zeke picked up an end table and smashed it through the street facing window. The tinkling glass drew the attention of an infected woman kneeling over L.C.'s still squirming body. Guilt nearly paralyzed Zeke as he climbed through the casement and dropped the seven feet to the ground. He knew there was nothing he could have done for L.C., and he couldn't have made it upstairs to help Meagan or Mildred and Lester, either. Still, he couldn't overcome having left them behind. Whether he could have helped them or not, he felt he had abandoned them.

A crawling infected man dragged himself toward Zeke, blood trailing behind him from the stumps of legs severed near the hip. As Zeke ran past, a hand stretched out, grasping for his legs. Teeth clacked harmlessly behind him and fetid breath escaped its lips in a hiss. Zeke rounded the side of the house, making for the thick tree line at the back of the property a hundred yards away.

Thirty feet from the edge of the woods, Zeke looked back at the house. His eyes locked onto Meagan who was hanging out the bedroom window on the second story. Her mouth was moving, but the noise of the helicopter, which had opened up on the house again, overpowered whatever she was saying. Zeke sprinted back to the house. His heart was pounding like a drum when he yelled at Meagan, "Can you jump?"

"It's too far!" she screamed above the sounds of the thumping rotors, booming canon, splintering wood, and howling infected. He knew she was right. It had to be eighteen or nineteen feet from the edge of the window to the ground. A broken or badly sprained ankle would mean near certain death.

"Is there any rope?" Zeke asked, desperately hoping for a way to get her out.

"No," she yelled frantically.

Zeke racked his brain for a way to rescue her. "Is there a bed?" he yelled back, an idea forming in his head.

"Yes," was the panicked reply. "I don't think I have much time."

"Take the sheets off the bed and tie the ends together."

"Why?"

"You're going to make a rope to climb down." A look of understanding suddenly appeared on her face. A workable plan of escape erased the crippling terror of impending doom that, moments before, had left her paralyzed with fear. She disappeared from view as she moved deeper into the room. Thirty seconds later, she reappeared in the window with sheets in her hand. In view of Zeke, she took the corners of the two sheets and tied them together.

"No," Zeke yelled up at the window. "You need to leave more at the end so you can double knot it. Otherwise, it will come apart when you put your weight on it."

She quickly undid the knot and retied it. This time there was enough material left at the end of the knot to tie a second. She pulled on the ends of the sheets and locked the knot tight. "What do I tie it to?" she asked looking around the room.

"You need something that is long enough to stretch across the window," he yelled back. "Is there a chair or something? It has to be strong enough to support your weight."

She disappeared again, returning ten seconds later. In her hand was a broom with a wooden handle. "Will this work?" she yelled down, her voice once again filling with panic. Having heard her voice, the infected, which had been feeding on Lester and Mildred in the adjacent room, were drawn to the bedroom and initiated an assault on the door, trying to bang their way into the room.

"They're trying to get in!" she screamed, tears once again cascading down her face in saline torrents.

Realizing they would breach the room any moment, Zeke put aside his doubts that the broom stick was strong enough to support her weight and, with as much reassurance as he could muster, affirmed that it would hold her. "Tie the sheet to the middle of the stick. Don't forget to double knot it."

Meagan worked feverishly, adrenaline making her fingers clumsy. In spite of her degraded fine motor skills, she completed the knot. Under normal circumstances, she would have easily worked out the next step, but under the terror of being eaten, she couldn't figure out what to do with the broom.

She stood at the window, looking uncertainly at the stick in her hands. Zeke realized she needed further direction. "Hold onto the stick and drop the sheets out the window." Without understanding his plan, she complied. The sheet rope cascaded down and was tugged to the side by the breeze, unfurling like a huge flag of surrender. "Put the stick across the window and make sure there's plenty protruding past either edge."

As he was yelling, the helicopter fired a short burst into the house. The rapid booming of the helicopter's canon covered his directions, so he shouted them out again.

As she placed the broom stick across the window, the physics of the plan clicked in her mind, and a look of understanding and confidence reappeared on her face. Keeping tension on the broom, she positioned herself in the window facing away from the room, sheet rope in her hands.

She paused, considering the best way to begin her rappelling climb downward. In a crash that Zeke could not hear, the infected broke through the door. Without warning, in a move that caused Zeke's teeth to tightly clench together in fear for her safety, she jumped outward, sheet sliding through her fingers. A tenth of a second later, she tightened her grip on the sheet, arresting her fall. The broom stick bowed outward under the weight, but refused to break.

What started as a straight fall powered by gravity turned into an arc toward the house as she swung inward on the sheet like the pendulum on a grandfather clock. Her body slammed into the side of the house with a jolting impact that crushed the air out of her lungs, and left her stunned. In spite of the pain, she refused to release her vice-like grip on the sheet. Her timidity and fear were unexpectedly replaced with a desire to live, a will to do whatever it took to stay alive. As she clung helplessly to the sheet, feet dangling ten feet above the ground, an inexplicable realization swept over her. She would survive. She would never again allow herself to be a helpless, passive victim of her circumstances. Hand over hand, she lowered herself down the sheet. Her feet sought purchase on the side of the house, but found nothing to take the weight and ease the burning in her forearms and biceps. She continued descending and fought past what she thought was her ultimate, endurable limit of fatigue. Finally, she reached the end of the sheet. Her feet were still five feet from the ground when she released her grasp and fell the rest of the way, landing with bent knees absorbing the joint-jarring shock of the impact.

Meagan looked up at the window to see a young man in his twenties eyeing her from the position she had just vacated. His furious voice chased after her as she followed Zeke to the tree line.

Looking over her shoulder, she saw the man leap from the window in pursuit. The earth's pull on his body created enough force to shatter both of his legs on impact. Undeterred by his inability to walk, he continued his pursuit, dragging himself on his elbows. Another body leaped from the window and then a third, fourth and fifth. The results were the same for each.

Zeke and Meagan reached the woods and disappeared into the thick, entangling mass of bushes, small trees, and kudzu. The sight of the nightmare behind them was quickly blotted out by dense foliage.

Chapter 23

Just after they entered the woods, a loud *whoosh* preceded an explosion. A second later, a concussion blasted through the woods, knocking leaves from the trees. Meagan felt the pressure wave slap her in the back, leaving her ears ringing. Wood debris from the house rained down around them, some pieces large enough to break branches off the nearby trees. A black column of smoke billowed into the blue sky. They didn't slow until they had traveled half a mile from the house.

Finally Zeke pulled up and stopped. Meagan, who had been staying right on his heels, stopped, too. Zeke bent over and supported the weight of his upper body by resting his hands on his knees. He grabbed gulping breaths of air, trying to restore the deficit of oxygen and rid his body of excess carbon dioxide.

Meagan was winded from the breakneck race over rough terrain, but not nearly to the extent that Zeke was. In an uncharacteristic show of calmness, she said, "I bet you're wishing you spent less of your gym time growing your arms and more of it working on cardio."

Zeke did a double take in response. Ten minutes ago, she shrieked in terror when one of the infected ran into the side of the house. Now she was calm and making jokes after having narrowly escaped being eaten and blown to bits.

"Yeah, I suppose a little extra cardio training would come in handy right now," he admitted suspiciously, wondering if she was undergoing some sort of mental breakdown. "Are you okay?" he asked.

"As good as can be expected," she answered. Her voice definitely contained emotion, but the debilitating panic from before had been replaced by an air of control. Knowing what he was really asking, she continued, "I don't know what happened to me. Something in me changed when I was climbing down the sheets. I know I've been really emotional since this started." She paused and looked at the ground in embarrassment. "That isn't me. I'm normally a very level headed person. When everything started, something snapped. I felt broken, like I couldn't handle what was happening. My family was infected and I was trapped in the city with nobody.

"When you included me in your group, I still felt helpless. I wasn't alone anymore, but I knew I was in way over my head. It kept getting worse until I was hanging from the sheet with those things in the room above fixing to eat me. In that moment, I realized I was the only one who could save myself. I can't explain it. I was suddenly overcome by the resolve to fight and to live. It was like God reached into my head in that instant and fixed whatever broke yesterday. The panic was gone."

She paused again, looking back at the plume of smoke writhing its way into the sky like a black snake. "I'm sorry about the cardio comment. It was pretty callous in light of everything that just happened. I guess I was feeling grateful to escape with my life and needed to say something to break the stress of the moment."

"Don't apologize. I'm just glad you're okay," he added,

still trying to figure out what had happened to her. Whatever it was, he wasn't going to complain. He wouldn't have survived another day with the Meagan of ten minutes ago. Her paralyzing panic attacks would have quickly gotten them both killed.

"We better keep moving," he finally said when he had managed to catch his breath.

"Where are we going?" Meagan asked.

"I don't know," Zeke confessed. "We need to get away from the state line though. I don't want to be mistaken for a sick person trying to cross the Alabama border. If we can make it back to Bowden, we might be able to find another car."

When they resumed their trek, Zeke led at a much slower pace. Although she didn't comment on it, he felt obliged to explain. "Now that we've put some distance between ourselves and whatever may be left of the Bowden Horde, I don't want to run ourselves to death. If we cross paths with more of them, we may have to run for our lives. I think it would be wise to move slowly enough to have an energy reserve available if we need it."

"That makes sense," she said in an even voice. Zeke had been huffing and puffing when he spoke. She was right. He should have spent more time on the cardio equipment. His muscle bulk was proving to be a hindrance to him. The extra weight was doing little more than tiring him.

They cautiously moved through woods, open pastures and more woods. Finally, after an hour, they circled back to the highway just west of Bowden.

"We need to find somewhere indoors where we can hole up for a while. I have one full magazine left and a couple rounds in the other. If we run out of bullets, we're in serious trouble," Zeke said as he looked left and right out of habit. There wasn't a car in sight. He slowly stepped onto the road with Meagan at his side.

Meagan carried a stick she had picked up in the woods. It was about three feet long and three inches thick. She had found it in the remains of a tree that had been cut for firewood. It was green wood and was very dense. It obviously wasn't the best weapon to use against the infected, but at least it was something. It kept her destiny in her own hands. It gave her the ability to fend for herself. She had no doubts that Zeke would do everything he could to protect her, including sacrificing his life. He hadn't hesitated to run back to the house which was full of infected and under fire from the helicopter. It wasn't in her nature to depend on others and to expect them to take care of her, though. She had always been self-sufficient. The club gave her the ability to remain that way; it enabled her to defend herself.

Nobody was driving on Highway 166. Everybody knew the Alabama state line was closed. There was nothing on the highway between Bowden and the state line except for a few farms. That, and the fact that the horde had gone that way, kept everybody off the road.

As Zeke and Meagan walked into Bowden, the town appeared deserted. There were no vehicles driving on the streets. An occasional dog barked, but other than that, the silence was ominous: no lawn mowers, no cars, no airplanes. Just silence. As the houses grew closer together on smaller lots, they occasionally saw a face peering around drawn curtains. Many of the faces disappeared as soon as they realized they had been seen.

"There's another one," Meagan pointed out as they walked passed a single story brick house. This face didn't disappear like the rest when her pointing finger indicated its presence. It didn't respond when she waved either. At first it just eyed them with morbid interest. Then the face banged into the window. Its head reared back and its mouth opened. A faint howl made its way through the negligible space between the closed window and the frame it slid in. The face behind the glass twisted and contorted in rage. A scream from the house across the street answered in reply. Closed curtains in a large window swayed back and forth as a body rubbed against them.

Zeke turned and saw two faces in a small kitchen window of another house. The faces mirrored the neighbor across the street in grimaces of rage. Another scream came from somewhere behind the first house. This one, however, didn't come from within a house. It rang out in a hauntingly clear vocalization that brought terror from the hidden recesses of Zeke's mind. It back brought images from horror movies he had watched late at night at slumber parties as a kid. It brought back images from Mutual of Omaha's Wild Kingdom he watched with his grandpa, images of predators about to pounce on their prey. The howls forebode impending death. He understood that the death the howls were announcing were his and Meagan's.

They broke into a run. Another unseen voice clearly belted out a demonic scream that pierced through both of them and spurred them on to greater speed. Even though the specters were as yet unseen, there was no doubt they were there. As they continued to run, they passed a body lying on the sidewalk. It had been picked apart; there was virtually no skin left on the body and very little muscle remained on the bones. A severed arm lay a short distance away from its torso. Tattered and ripped clothing was strewn about the corpse, further evidence of what was lurking out of sight.

The road curved slightly. As they rounded the bend, Bowden High School came into view. "We need to get off this road and get inside," Zeke wheezed as he struggled to satisfy his body's screaming demands for oxygen. His legs were wobbly, and his vision was spotty; exhaustion was threatening to send him to his knees. His forward progress was fueled solely by adrenaline and a stubborn refusal to give up and die. Meagan was huffing beside him. She may have been in better shape than him, but she was struggling now as well. Both were near the point of complete exhaustion.

The school seemed like the best immediate option for a secure indoor location to rest. Screaming voices grew around them. There were at least a dozen keeping pace with them, possibly on parallel streets. "I can't go much further," Meagan gasped as they approached the school's entrance. Zeke pulled on the handle. The door was locked. He looked through the narrow, wire-impregnated glass, trying to see inside. The hallway was dark and empty.

He turned from the door and saw two bodies emerge from around the bend two or three hundred yards behind. The two men stopped, eyeing them without moving. Even from that distance, the absence of other noise permitted sound to carry clearly when one of the men took a snorting breath, sampling the air with its nose.

"We're out of time," Zeke said, voicing the obvious. He resumed his flight in search of another door that might permit them entrance to the building. When he looked over his shoulder, the infected men broke into a pursuing sprint.

Zeke and Meagan rounded the corner of the building. They passed a worksite where somebody had been painting a huge red *B* on the side of the building. The job had been abandoned without any effort at clean up. A ladder still leaned against the wall.

As Zeke passed the neglected equipment, Meagan, who was several paces behind, yelled, "Wait!" Zeke spun on his heels. Meagan had already started extending the aluminum ladder. He understood what she was doing without being told. If one door was locked, they were probably all locked. If they couldn't get safely inside, they could at least get on the roof and out of reach, assuming the ladder was tall enough. The ladder clinked rapidly as the locking mechanism slid over each rung and was pulled back into place by spring tension. At maximum extension, the ladder was a good five feet short of the roof. Before Zeke had a chance to make sure the legs were securely positioned on the ground, Meagan was already ascending two rungs at a time; any trepidation or signs of caution were afterthoughts she didn't have time to consider.

Zeke bounded up the rungs behind her, catching the back of her shoe in the mouth as he climbed. The ladder bowed under the weight of the two scalers roughly climbing at the same time. Meagan blatantly ignored the sticker which warned to refrain from using the top rung. Placing her hands against the wall for balance, she stepped onto the top rung, stretched upward, and wrapped her fingers over the ledge of the roof. She pushed off the ladder as she pulled with her arms to give the slight acceleration needed to overcome her dead weight and pull herself up. The push off caused the ladder to teeter slightly and it began a slow motion succumbence to gravity. Two rungs from the top, Zeke tried to steady the ladder by pushing his hands against the wall. His best efforts couldn't stop the ladder's slow leaning tilt.

Unable to stop the lean, he realized the ladder's fate was sealed. It was going to fall and unless he got off, he would fall with it. He stepped onto the second to last rung, raising the center of gravity, which increased the rate it slid across the side of the building. His only chance was to push off the rung with his legs and hopefully achieve enough height to reach the edge. His rubbery legs thrust upwards with every bit of strength they held in reserve. His arms stretched up, and both hands firmly grasped the ledge above him. In a fleeting thought, he realized that without the ladder, they wouldn't have a way to get off the roof. His foot reached out to the left and he wrapped the toe of his shoe around the top rung of the ladder, stopping its arcing path along the side of the building.

He looked to his right as Meagan pulled herself up onto the roof, two feet away. Looking to the left, he saw three infected tear around the corner. He pointed his feet up as far as he could with the ladder hooked at his ankles and pulled with his arms. He dragged his torso over the edge of the roof, but with the ladder dangling from his feet, he couldn't get his legs over the ledge. Meagan lay down on the ledge beside him, her head and arms hanging down, grasping for the top of the ladder. Zeke pulled his legs up as high as he could. Meagan touched it with her fingers, but couldn't get them around it. She scooted further over the edge until she reached the point she felt like there wasn't enough friction between her body and the roof to hold her in place. Zeke strained to pull his legs up higher. With a final grunt from Zeke, the ladder rose into her straining fingers.

She tried to pull it up, but only succeeded in pulling herself further over the edge. "Don't let go of it!" she screamed. "I can't hold on to both the roof and the ladder!"

With Meagan supporting part of the weight, Zeke pulled himself up far enough to swing his left leg over the top of the roof with the ladder still supported by his right foot. His body was now parallel to the edge of the roof. He maneuvered his body so that his weight was resting on Meagan's butt, pushing her down onto the roof. "I'm letting go with my foot. If you can't hold it, let go."

With Zeke's body pinning her to the roof, she was able to hold the ladder's full weight. She struggled to pull it upward as the small band of infected rapidly shortened the distance between themselves and the bottom of the ladder, which was now suspended three feet above the ground.

"Don't let it go, I've got you now," Zeke said as he repositioned himself to pull her away from the edge. As soon as he lifted his weight from her, she began to slide toward the edge.

"Don't let me go!" she screamed as her body slipped on the slick metal sheeting that covered the top of the building. He dropped to his belly and grabbed onto the waist band of her pants as she slid over the edge.

"Let go of the ladder. I can't hold you!" he yelled. The combined weight of Meagan and the ladder pulled him across the smooth surface. Meagan refused to let the ladder fall. The realization that he couldn't support her weight without being pulled off the roof himself stung like a hornet. He refused to let go of her as he slid closer to the edge of the roof. As he reached the point where hope was lost, something snagged on his belt, stopping the forward progression that was going to end with the two of them plummeting to the ground. "Let it go!" he yelled again, struggling to hang onto her. Her body hung vertically, head first over the edge of the roof. Zeke was holding onto her thighs, but they were sliding through his grasp. She still refused to let it go.

"Bend your lower leg toward the ground," he grunted. She obeyed, bending them so far that her feet touched her butt. The sharp angle in her legs provide a solid hand hold and her legs quit sliding through his hands.

Afraid to break loose from whatever had snagged his belt and had created the tenuous state of equilibrium holding them on the roof, Zeke hesitated to haul her up. After a second had passed and the snag showed no signs of letting go, he started pulling. He pulled her up as far as he could and then released his right hand and grabbed onto the waist of her jeans and pulled her further toward the roof.

Her feet squirmed, kicking him in the face for the second time in a matter of seconds as they sought something solid. His biceps burned as he pulled her dangling body back over the lip of the building, the ladder still in her hands. Finally he brought her to the point where only her arms hung toward the ground, still clutching the ladder. He let go of her waist band and edged himself to the lip of the roof, pulling the ladder out of reach as the first infected arrived with up stretched arms, grasping for the bottom rung which was just beyond its fingertips.

Zeke doubted they would have been able to climb it, but if one of them latched onto it, he and Meagan would have lost it forever. With both of their feet firmly planted on the roof, pulling the ladder the rest of the way up was a simple task. Once it lay securely on the roof, Zeke and Meagan took a minute to simply sit down and regain their breath.

When he was finally able to speak, Zeke looked at the hex headed roofing screw that had snagged his belt. With a forced smile, he said, "And that's why I spent the extra time doing reps of curls instead of working on my cardio."

Chapter 24

The clamor at the bottom of the building increased in volume and intensity. In mere minutes, more and more individuals heeded the feeding call of the first three infected that had chased Zeke and Meagan up the roof. They ran to the building from all directions, fighting for position around the area where Meagan kept peering down at the growing mob.

After an hour, the clouds began to break. With the disappearance of the clouds, the dark metal roof began to heat up. Sitting on the sun scorched metal quickly became unthinkable. The temperature cut through the cushioned soles of Zeke's running shoes as he stood. Meagan's tennis shoes were thicker soled, but only offered a slight reprieve from the blistering heat that was cooking her feet.

The thick Georgia air was saturated with moisture. The ninety percent humidity prevented the drenching sweat from evaporating and offering any cooling effect. "If we don't get off this roof soon, we're going to die. Without water, we won't make it through a day."

"What's the point?" Meagan questioned dejectedly. "If we leave the roof, the mob is going to eat us. I'd rather die up here from the heat than be torn apart and eaten alive down there."

Zeke shook his head as his foot ran back and forth over another of the hex headed screws that held the metal roofing panels in place. "It doesn't have to be die up here or die down there. There has to be another option," he said. "There's always another option!"

"Our problem is we climbed onto the wrong roof. If we got on that building, we could have broken out the skylight and gotten inside," she lamented as she pointed at the building thirty feet away where the dark tint of the plastic skylight was plainly visible.

"Maybe we can still get on that roof," Zeke said hopefully, an idea formulating in his head. "If you could get all the infected to gather on the far side of the building, I could lower the ladder to the ground and you could run over to this side. We could climb down, move the ladder to that building, and climb up before they realize what's happening."

Meagan's face lit up in a smile. "I love it when a plan comes together."

"Hannibal Smith, The A Team," Zeke said, laughing. "I haven't heard that one for a while. I didn't know girls liked The A Team."

Meagan laughed as they walked to the side of the roof that was opposite from the other building. "When I was little, my dad and I watched it together all the time. I had a huge crush on Face when I was ten years old."

"That figures," Zeke said, smiling. As they walked the edge of the roof, fifty or sixty bodies screamed and wailed angrily on the ground. The group followed them step for step, nineteen feet below. Every five or six steps, Zeke banged noisily on the side of the building yelling, "Come and get it!" The agitated group continued to grow as more individuals ran to the discordant commotion. The large group of infected below them followed in a raucous commotion of moans and howls as Zeke and Meagan led them away from where Zeke was going to lower the ladder.

"I think we have a problem, Zeke. You're banging is drawing them from all over the city." Zeke had been looking at the growing number below him. When he looked up, he realized that infected were streaming in from all over town, drawn by the noise he was making as well as the wails from the hungry mouths below.

"We can't catch a break for anything," he muttered despondently, as he stopped and stared at the small groups and individual infected running toward the mob below him.

"It may not be as bad as it seems," Meagan disagreed. "They're all coming to this side of the building where we're making noise. Get ready with the ladder and I'm going to keep their attention over here. When you're ready, I'll move away from the edge and meet you on the other side and we'll make a break for it."

Zeke slowly backed out of sight and Meagan began banging on the side of the building. She realized that the banging probably wasn't even necessary as long as they could see her. The sight of a meal was all that was really needed to hold the attention of all the eyes focused on her with rapt attention. She turned to see how Zeke was coming.

He picked up the ladder with a soft clang as the end bumped into an air conditioning unit sitting upright on the flat of the roof. The noise wasn't that loud, but several of the infected suddenly seemed to have lost their fascination with Meagan and their gaze shifted away from her toward the roof in the middle of the building. Although Zeke had backed away from the edge and was out of sight, the noise was enough to pique their curiosity. A group of eight moved to the middle of the building, staring up at the roof where the noise had originated.

"Try to keep the noise down," Meagan yelled. "That bang attracted a small group to directly below where you hit the air conditioner."

Zeke silently nodded to her, signifying he would keep quiet. He traversed the rest of the roof without making any noise. By the time he had cautiously made his way to the far end, the small group that had been drawn by the sound had lost interest and returned to the main body.

Zeke began to lower the ladder over the side as carefully and quietly as he could, but as the extended ladder slid across the edge of the roof and down toward the ground, it rattled and clanked softly. At the first rattle, the same group of eight infected once again lost interest in Meagan. The soft metallic screech of the ladder sliding across the edge of the roof started the group in his direction.

"Quiet, Zeke," Meagan chided. "They're coming your way." She jumped, yelled, waved her arms, and banged on the side of the building.

The small group that had splintered off stopped their advance toward Zeke who was holding the ladder motionless at the far side of the building, but they didn't return to the main group. They continued to look back and forth from Zeke's end of the building to Meagan's, as if unable to make up their mind whether to investigate the unknown noise or return to a sure quarry that Meagan represented.

For five minutes, they stood in indecision before they once again started moving toward Zeke, despite his silence.

As soon as they rounded the corner, Zeke and the ladder came into view. They moaned in delight at finding another potential meal. The moans quickly turned into irritated wails at the realization that he was out of reach. The sound drew twenty more bodies from the main group.

"It's no good," Meagan yelled to him. "There's a bunch more coming to your side."

Zeke pulled the ladder back up and dropped it onto the roof in anger. Meagan drew back from the far edge and walked to Zeke.

"I thought it was going to work," she said dispiritedly as she looked across the narrow expanse to the sky lights on the far building that had offered a promised entrance inside and a reprieve from the blistering heat.

Zeke set the ladder on its edge and they sat on it in silence for several minutes. The realization slowly set in that unless the infected below them suddenly lost interest and left, they were going to die of exposure on the roof.

As Meagan stared at a row of screw heads sticking up a quarter inch above the metal, she dolefully said it was too bad they didn't have some tools to take out the roofing screws and remove a piece of metal sheeting because they could use the sheets to make a lean-to shade against the air conditioning unit.

"Why didn't I think of that?" Zeke asked rhetorically. "We might be able to do better than make a shade. If we can take a sheet of the metal off, we might be able to whittle through the wood sheeting beneath and get into the building. He quickly pulled a multi-tool from his pocket and unfolded it, gaining access to the pliers. He set to work twisting the small hex heads of the screws. It was laborious and tedious work, but one by one, they slowly backed out.

He and Meagan switched off every few minutes. Sweat dripped from their skin, landing on the sheet of metal they were removing, forming miniature streams that ran down the metal valleys before evaporating and adding to the humidity. After nearly twenty minutes, they had removed all the screws in a twelve foot long panel. Pulling it aside revealed the plywood underneath. Zeke quickly opened the knife blade and began poking and scraping at the wood surface.

In short order, he managed to whittle an inch-wide hole through the wood. With a hole started, he closed the knife blade and opened the three inch saw blade. As he rapidly worked it up and down, he looked up at Meagan and said, "Up until now, I have always considered the saw the most worthless attachment on this thing. Now, if I could find the designer who included it in the tool, I would give him a thousand bucks for his genius." His pace slowed as fatigue set in.

"Let me take a turn," Meagan said excitedly. The prospect of getting out of the sun had lightened her dreary mood considerably. They switched places and she began the up and down motion, extending the six-inch line Zeke had cut in the roof.

When her steady pace began to waver, they traded places again. The smell of freshly cut wood spurred them on as the cut steadily grew until it was two feet long. "Do you figure that's long enough?" Meagan inquired as they switched again and she took the tool from Zeke.

"I think so," he stated as she took the knife blade out and whittled another round hole so she could begin a new cut ninety degrees away from the first.

In a little over thirty minutes they had nearly completed

a two foot by two foot square hole. With six inches left to cut, Zeke stood and stomped on the middle of the cutout. The remainder of the uncut wood broke in a ragged edge, opening a hole to the interior of the building. The square of wood fell four feet where it landed on a layer of insulation covering the top of a drop ceiling. Supporting himself with an arm resting on either side of the hole, Zeke cautiously lowered himself into it. His feet touched the surface below and he allowed more weight to come to bear on it. It suddenly gave way as the ceiling tile cracked under his weight and fell to the floor below. "What do you think?" he asked. "If we drop the ladder down, we should be able to get inside."

"Better make sure there aren't any infected in there before we blindly climb down."

He lowered himself back into the hole and stomped his feet up and down, knocking several more tiles out of the frame and pulled himself back up to the roof.

After yelling for a minute straight, nothing came into view of the expanded hole beneath them. "I guess it's probably okay," Meagan said. Together they picked up the ladder and lowered it into the hole. When it was as low as they could reach, Zeke laid on the roof and reaching down, lowered it the final three feet to the tile floor and rested the top against the side of the hole he had knocked out of the drop ceiling.

Zeke pulled his pistol out of his holster and lowered himself into the hole again, his feet roving back and forth, wildly searching for the ladder. When they were firmly planted on the top rung, he exclaimed, "Here goes nothing," and lowered himself down.

The air between the roof and the drop ceiling was full of

stirred up insulation. As he climbed through the void, his skin began itching as the tiny particles settled into the pores of his exposed skin. Meagan watched breathlessly as he descended into the interior of the school.

With both feet firmly planted on the floor, he looked around, put the gun back in the holster, and placed his hands firmly on the sides of the ladder to steady it. "I have the ladder, come on down," he yelled up.

Meagan's leg trembled as her foot searched blindly for the first rung. Finding it, her second foot instantly made contact and her first foot stepped down to the second rung, her hands cautiously maintaining a steadying grip on the outer roof. With her second foot securely planted on the second rung, one hand timidly let go of the roof and then shot down to the support of the ladder. Once both hands were on the ladder, her confidence increased and she rapidly descended to the floor, coming down between Zeke's arms which were still holding the ladder in support. With both feet on the floor, Zeke let go of the ladder. Meagan turned around and wrapped her arms around him. Their sweat drenched shirts clung together as she hugged him and pulled their bodies into tight contact.

"I thought we were going to die up there," she said as she released him from her embrace and reveled in the relative coolness of the building.

"So did I," he said. "But as good as being off the roof is, if you turn around, there's something even better behind you."

Meagan turned cautiously, not wanting to get her hopes up as she tried to imagine what could be better than escaping the convection broiler where they had spent the last three hours. On the wall directly behind her was a water fountain. "Ladies first," Zeke said as she bent over and the cool water ran across her cracked lips and down her parched throat.

Chapter 25

The building they had broken into turned out to be the administrative building. A cursory glance down the white hallway showed offices on either side, and halfway down the hall a sign indicated the teacher's room. Beyond that were walls lined with blue lockers stacked two tall.

As they walked toward the far end of the hallway, Zeke tried each door knob. None yielded to the twisting force he applied. At the end of the hall was the double door through which he had first attempted to enter the building. Both doors had a crash bar which he carefully avoided pushing as he put his face to the narrow window and peered through the tinted glass at the crowd milling around outside. His actions on the roof had formed the second Bowden Horde. It was just as large as the first and they showed no signs of losing interest.

"Let me see your tool again," Meagan said. He handed it to her and she opened the knife blade. Zeke turned back to the window and continued to look despondently at the mass of bodies waiting to sink their teeth into his flesh. His attention was drawn away from the window by a metallic *click*. He looked back for the source of the noise and saw Meagan pull a door open, revealing rows of four foot wide counters inside a classroom. Each counter had a sink with a long curved faucet at one end. On the other end of the counter, there was a conical spigot with a chrome handle. He recognized the spigots from his days in high school and college chemistry. They provided methane gas for the Bunsen burners.

Meagan walked across the hallway and slipped the knife blade between the door jamb and the door. The point speared the latch. Working the knife from side to side, she was able to push the latch into the door and pull the door open. Inside was another classroom. This one had rows of tables, each with two chairs neatly pushed in, facing the front of the room. Along a counter in the back were jars of pickled animals and organs. The next room they opened housed what appeared to be the physics lab.

The building had been constructed in the 70's when the educational theory stated that the classroom should be devoid of all distractions from the outside world. In an effort to achieve that goal, the classrooms had small windows just below the ceiling. They let natural light into the room and provided ventilation when opened, but were too high to permit students to see more than the sky outside. In order to maintain a uniform appearance in architecture, the offices had the same window configuration.

The short-lived, bad idea in the ever-changing world of educational philosophy was cemented in time by the architecture of schools built during the era. Bad as the philosophy was, it turned out to be a life saver for anybody trying to find refuge in a school built during that time. In this case, it kept Zeke and Meagan out of reach and sight of the infected outside. The windows were too high to allow them to gain entrance into the building.

Meagan worked her magic one more time on the door

across the hall from the physics lab. The sign on the door read "Teachers' Room." The spacious room had two cheaply made, large, round tables at one end. The tables were surrounded by molded plastic chairs with shiny chrome legs. Two silver refrigerators and an upright freezer adorned the wall space nearest the tables. To the left side of the refrigerators was a vending machine full of candy. Flanking it was another with drinks. A flat screen television hung from one wall. At the other end of the room, an oak pool table, an air hockey table, and a foosball table occupied the central space. A row of computers lined the back wall, each in a partitioned off section of a long table.

Zeke whistled as he took in the room. "It must be rough teaching in this school." As he walked to the vending machine, he added, "I don't think I'd ever leave the teacher's room if I worked here."

The contents of the vending machine alone would keep them fed for at least a week. In addition to the junk food, the refrigerators contained a substantial stash of real food and a pile of sack lunches that were left when teachers fled the school. There were enough bags of lettuce to make salad for several days. Zeke picked up a gallon size jug, sloshing milk around the top of the nearly full container, as he lifted it to examine the expiration date. "Good for two more weeks," he proclaimed. Somebody must have made their daily breakfast on the stove because there was enough bacon and eggs to produce a statin requiring spike in cholesterol levels of three large men.

Zeke pulled the handle on the freezer door. As the door opened, frigid air rolled out, colliding with the warm air of the teachers' room. When the two air masses collided, a steamy cloud of vapor formed, rolling and swirling at the edges.

Zeke pulled out a clear vacuum sealed bag with a warning message written in black sharpie: "Hands off, G. Howe." Holding up the half pound package of frozen meat, "It looks like we're having steak tonight," Zeke proclaimed. "And tomorrow night," he added as he held up a second package, "And the next night," as he held up a third package. With his hands full of meat, he smiled and said, "It looks like we're going to be having steak all week. I hope G. Howe doesn't mind."

Zeke dug a handful of change out of his pocket and *clinked* seventy-five cents into the shiny coin slot in the face of the vending machine. He pushed the button with a picture of a bottle of Gatorade next to it. The innards of the machine *thumped* and *thudded* softly until a twenty ounce bottle made its way out of the machine, landing in the black holder near the bottom with a *clunk*.

Zeke picked up the bottle, refreshingly cool in his hand, sat down at the table, and said, "Pull up a chair and I'll share."

Meagan pulled out a chair beside him, and enthusiastically answered, "You've got yourself a date, Mister."

Zeke took a long draw from the mouth of the bottle and pushed it across the table toward Meagan. She lifted it to her mouth and didn't set it down until it was half empty. She wiped her mouth with the back of her hand and slid it back to Zeke.

While Meagan was taking her second nip at the bottle, Zeke reached across the table for the slender black remote and turned on the TV. When the screen lit up, it was tuned to CNN. "That figures," he chided.

"What figures?" Meagan asked.

"That the TV in the teacher's lounge is tuned in to the *Communist News Network*."

"You're saying that teachers are liberal because the TV was tuned to CNN?" she asked accusingly.

"Hey, if the shoe fits," he answered.

She grabbed the remote from him as she said, "My mom and sister are teachers. They're the most conservative people you'd ever meet." She pushed the recall button on the remote and the TV switched to Fox News. "It looks to me like the teachers here are conservative and the janitor is the liberal one," she countered as she set the remote back on the table. She sat looking at the TV and then let out a long breath, "Liberal, conservative, it doesn't matter anymore. With all that's happening out there, nobody is going to care about politics anymore. At this point in history, we're all just people trying to survive."

Zeke nodded in silent agreement without turning from the TV. He watched for a couple minutes and turned it off. "Nothing's changed. I don't have it in me to watch any more of that. We've been living it all day."

Zeke visited the drink machine again, expending the last of the change from his pocket. "I guess that's it for the drinks. I'm not sure how to break into the machine."

"I don't think you'll have to," Meagan said, standing on her tip toes and stretching to get a metal coffee can from the top of one of the refrigerators. She reached in and as she pulled her hand out, allowed a stream of quarters to flow between her fingers and *clink* back into the nearly full can. "Think anybody will mind if we raid the coffee fund?" she giggled.

"I hate to take coffee from anybody's cup," he said sarcastically. "We'll leave IOUs for every dime we take." Becoming more serious he added, "With all of your not-so-secret admirers out there, I think we may be stuck here for a while. Do you want to explore the rest of the building before dinner and see if there's anything else of value to us?"

Having had a chance to cool down and rehydrate, Zeke and Meagan left the teacher's room and continued opening locked doors as they proceeded down the hallway. For the most part, the rooms proved to be an uninteresting assortment of offices. The second to last room was identified by a sign on the door as the sick room. When the door was opened, Meagan was pleased to see that either side of the room had a single bed with crisp looking white sheets.

She smiled and said, "This may be the best find so far. I was afraid I was going to have to sleep on the floor."

"That's great," Zeke said. "For the past two days, I've been worried about getting eaten alive and trying to keep you from being torn to pieces and all you've been worried about is having to sleep on the floor. I'll never understand the female mind."

Meagan punched him in the arm. "That's not what I meant. I'm just glad to have an occasional reminder of the finer things in life."

"A bed that doesn't even have a blanket qualifies as one of the finer things in life? If you're that easy to keep happy, I should marry you right now."

"Sorry to burst you bubble, but I'm only twenty-two and since I was about five years old, my dad has told me I'm not even allowed to date until I'm thirty-five. You're gonna have to wait for thirteen years." As soon as she said it, her head dropped, her infectious smile vanished, and tears began welling up in her eyes.

Zeke cautiously wrapped his arm around her shoulder in an awkward attempt to comfort her. Accepting his half-hearted embrace, Meagan wrapped both of her arms around him and for the second time in two days, buried her head in his chest and wept.

Chapter 26

In less than a minute, Meagan was wiping the tears from her eyes and apologizing. "I'm sorry for losing it again. I keep forgetting my parents are gone," she said, sniffling. "My dad and I were really close. Talking about him reminded me that he's gone." She inhaled again, the loose mucus in her nose gurgling as air passed through it and sucked it further up into her sinus passages.

"Don't worry about it. I understand," Zeke said, trying to comfort her and surprisingly not minding her exhibitions of emotion. "I'll give you two more outbursts and then you're going to have to keep it together."

Meagan laughed and said, "Thanks. That's really generous of you." Tears continued draining from her eyes and into her sinuses and nose, resulting in the formation of more snot than she could contain. Embarrassed, she turned away from Zeke, pulled the front of the shirt up to her face and blew her nose on the fabric.

"That has to be the most repulsive thing I have ever seen. And in light of what I have experienced during the last day, that's saying a lot," Zeke asserted, feigning disgust as she turned around.

Zeke's response caused the capillaries in her face to open up, raising the temperature of her skin and turning it a rosy hue of red. "I'm sorry. I can't believe I just did that in front of you," she uttered in humiliation.

"This definitely takes our relationship to a new level. I think this means I can fart in front of you now," Zeke teased with a twinkle in his eye.

"Uhh, no! You will never be allowed to fart in my presence," she said as her face once again lit up and the excess blood drained away, removing the previous sign of embarrassment. She grabbed onto the bend in his arm and pulled him to the last door. "Let's see if there's anything worthwhile behind lucky door number thirteen." Slipping the blade of her knife between the latch and the door, she quickly circumvented the lock.

"I'd say this one is worthwhile," Zeke exclaimed excitedly. The last door opened into the maintenance shop. Sitting in one of the bays was a red pickup truck. He loped across the shop and pulled the door open. The interior of the truck dinged, indicating the keys were in the ignition. Sliding into the seat, he twisted the key forward. The engine growled to life without hesitation.

Zeke looked over the gauges and stuck his head out the open door, happily proclaiming, "It has a full tank of gas! We're in business."

"That's great. Now why don't you turn it off before you poison us with carbon monoxide?"

"Fair enough. I want to check on your admirer's outside and see if they're losing interest anyway," he answered.

Encouraged by the presence of a vehicle, especially one with a full tank of fuel, Zeke quickly traversed the length of the hallway and peered out the window. The area in front of the building was still full of infected, standing room only.

Meagan stood beside him and looked out the window in

the opposite door. "There are just as many as an hour ago. Why aren't they leaving?"

"Who knows? Maybe they don't have a reason to go anywhere else. Right here is probably just as good as wherever they were before. This does present an interesting opportunity, though."

"How can this be an opportunity?" she asked dubiously.

"With all the noise we made up there, I suspect we attracted most of the free infected in town and now they're all huddled in a tight group right outside the front door. We have an opportunity to help out the town by killing them all with a single *BANG!*" he said enthusiastically as he clapped his hands together. "We have everything we need right behind you in the chemistry lab."

"Do you know anything about chemistry?" she asked doubtfully.

"I should," he answered excitedly. "When I was in college, I doubled majored. Chemistry was my second major. I have just the thing in mind. Have you ever heard of TATP?"

"No, I can't say that I have. What is it?"

"Triacetone Triperoxide, or TATP, is a high order explosive that's made from chemicals found in every basic chemistry storeroom. It's unusual among explosives because it doesn't contain any nitrogenous compounds. The other thing that makes it unusual is that its decomposition isn't exothermic or heat producing. The instability of the molecule comes from weak bonds between oxygen atoms within the molecule. When these bonds are stressed by shock or heat, they catastrophically break apart. A single molecule of TATP rapidly breaks down into a molecule of ozone and three molecules of acetone in its gaseous state. The four new gas molecules take up a lot more space than the original molecule which was in the solid state. The decomposition creates a shockwave as the new molecules are forced outward. The force of one molecule decomposing into four gaseous molecules is enough to cause all the other TATP molecules to explosively break down at the same time. All of the molecules coming apart at once create a huge blast. The explosion is eighty-three percent as strong as an equal amount of TNT, so it's pretty powerful stuff." Zeke paused as he transitioned from instructor mode back to conversation mode. "Unless you have something more pressing to do, I was thinking of whipping up a batch this evening."

"Do you even know how to make it?" she asked with notable skepticism in her voice.

"Does the pope wear a funny hat?" he asked.

Meagan stared at him blankly.

"Yes, I know how to make it. I probably made fifty batches of it in college. It was our Saturday night study break ritual. As long as the weather was good, we would make a couple ounces in the lab and then go set it off somewhere out in the countryside."

With her eyebrows raised questioningly, she asked, "What are we going to do with it?"

"We're going to blow it up," he said, unable to restrain the glee in his voice.

"Are we going to need blasting caps to set it off?" The more she heard, the more uncomfortable she was becoming.

"Blasting caps?" he laughed. "No way. This stuff is super unstable. The first time I made it, I was a TA for the high school chemistry teacher. I started it after school one day. The next day I went in to finish it while Mr. Robertson was at lunch. I was just about to pour the beaker through a filter to separate out the crystals when the door opened. I thought it was the teacher and spilled half the beaker on the counter. It turned out it wasn't the teacher, but I got spooked. Instead of doing a proper cleanup, I wiped it up with paper towels and tossed them in the garbage can. I didn't think about it at the time, but the paper towels picked up all the crystals from the countertop as well as the acid solution.

"Back then I didn't know anything about chemistry. I made it using an internet recipe I downloaded in the *Anarchist Cookbook*. It turns out the recipe was no good and the stuff was way too unstable. I was lucky I didn't blow my fingers off.

"Anyway, the trash can didn't get emptied over the weekend and the crystals dried out and decomposed. Monday morning, Mr. Robertson came into class and tossed an old printer ribbon cartridge into the trash can from across the room. The crystals were so unstable they only required a small vibration to set them off. The three point ribbon shot was more than enough. The explosion split the trash can in half and blew out the closest window. Luckily, Mr. Robertson was across the room and didn't get hurt. I heard about it later that day and didn't make any more TATP until I was in college and had the knowledge to do it safely, or at least relatively safely."

Zeke was all grins by the time he was finished with the story. The memories it brought back greatly improved what had been a dreary outlook minutes before.

"What do you need me to do?" Meagan questioned, not

really sure she even wanted to be part of the science experiment Zeke was proposing.

"That door over there has to be the chemical store room. Go do your thing on the lock so I can get the chemicals I need to get started."

"I wish I could, but my magic won't work on that door. It has a latch guard. Apparently word of your high school chemistry exploits must have made it all the way across the country."

"That figures. The educational system is hard at work to prevent imaginative boys from fully appreciating the wonders of what you can do with chemistry. It looks like we're going have to do this the old fashioned way. I'll be right back." Zeke disappeared from the classroom, his running footfalls echoing down the hall way only to slap their way back moments later. When he entered the chemistry room, he had a hammer in one hand and a chisel in the other.

"Are you going to chisel the latch out of the door?" she asked suspiciously.

"No, nothing so draconian as that," he answered ruefully as he used the hammer and chisel to first knock the lower hinge pin out of the door, and then the upper pin. The door teetered as its weight rested precariously on the latch and the unsecured hinges.

"Step aside, if you don't mind."

As Meagan moved to the left, Zeke placed the chisel behind the hinge and leveraged it outward until the door tilted slightly in the frame. The door hung, momentarily seesawing. Then Newton and his apples took over and the whole thing came crashing down, nearly crushing Zeke's toes into a pulpy mess as the weight of the solid oak door took a gouge from the floor a mere quarter inch from the end of his shoe.

Zeke smiled at the metal shelf lined with large, brown glass bottles. He ran his finger over the labels, examining each as he went. Grabbing three from various locations on the shelf, he enthusiastically roared, "This should get us started," as he set them down on the counter. "Hydrochloric acid, peroxide, and acetone: just what the doctor ordered."

"You're into this way too much. Should I be calling the FBI right now?" Meagan warily asked.

"If the FBI were to show up, we could skip this whole process. Why don't you see if they can come on over and rescue us?" Zeke said as he poured a clear liquid into a large graduated cylinder, carefully eyeing the level as it slowly climbed past line after line, making its way up the glass sides of the container. "That ought to do," he said, bending down so his eye was level with the meniscus, making sure it was exactly where he wanted it.

He poured the liquid into a larger beaker and set it aside and repeated the process with the other two bottles. With the measuring done, he took the beakers into the teacher's room and placed them in the freezer. As the liquids were cooling, he returned to the classroom and brought a cart full of supplies from the chemistry lab into the teacher's room.

"Why are you bringing the lab into the teacher's room?" Meagan questioned.

"I figured I could work on the bomb while I cook up a couple steaks for dinner. Personally, I've always found it a lot easier to cook dinner on the stove than over a Bunsen burner. Besides, the atmosphere is way better in here than in the lab. Half of a good steak dinner is the atmosphere in which you eat it."

Ten minutes later, with the aid of a spatula, Zeke scooped two sizzling steaks from the pan and flopped each one onto a plate beside the salad Meagan had prepared. "I don't know about you, but I'm starved," he said, sliding Meagan's plate in front of where she sat at the table.

After dinner, Zeke combined the chemicals and put them in an ice bath which he placed in one of the refrigerators. "That should do it for the bomb until tomorrow."

The next afternoon, he dumped the contents of the large beakers into coffee filters which collected white crystals as the liquid drained through. "We'll let these dry over night and by tomorrow, they should be ready to go -- or maybe I should say, ready to blow."

Chapter 27

That evening, Zeke and Meagan sat down to another dinner, each with one of G. Howe's steaks, salad, and a soda in front of them. There hadn't been a lot of food to cook, but a half pound steak was more than enough to fill the hollow feeling in their stomachs that candy bars hadn't satisfied during the day.

"You would think that G. Howe would at least have a decent steak knife to cut these prime pieces of meat," Meagan said in frustration as she struggled to cut her three-quarter inch steak with a butter knife.

"Try this," Zeke said, handing her his multi-tool which he had been using to cut his own meat.

"That's more like," she said as the blade sliced through the meat, blood seeping from the pink center. "It's hard to believe we're sitting here eating steak while the world is falling apart around us. I hardly ever ate steak when the world was going along the way it was supposed to."

After dinner, Meagan suggested turning on the news to see what was happening. Zeke picked up the remote and mashed the power button down with his finger. The TV clicked as the circuitry activated. The screen remained dark for several seconds while it warmed up. Eventually, an arrangement of colored bars appeared, replacing the black screen. A high pitched tone convinced Zeke to push the mute button. A message scrolled across the bottom of the screen, indicating to viewers that the station was off the air.

Zeke hit the recall button to switch to CNN. It was the same. He rapidly scrolled through the channels, searching for something with news. A handful of channels were broadcasting, but they were merely playing programs that had been locked into a computer days, or even weeks, before. There was nothing live on any of the stations.

"This isn't a good sign," Meagan said flatly. "If all the big news stations are down, it's truly falling apart out there. It has to be even worse than we've imagined."

Zeke nodded his head in silent agreement as he flipped through the channels one more time to make sure he hadn't missed anything. He hadn't. They still showed the same screen with colored bars and some type of no transmission message.

Meagan stood up suddenly, nearly knocking her chair over in her haste. "I saw a radio in one of the offices. Maybe there's a radio station that's still broadcasting." Zeke followed her down the hall into the office. It was an antiquated unit with analogue controls. She took it off the wall, placed it on the desk, and sat in the principal's plush leather chair. Zeke sat across the desk from her in the chair reserved for troubled youth in need of guidance. Suspecting he was probably well acquainted with the chair opposite the principal, she made a joking comment about his seeming familiarity with where he sat.

"Hmm," Zeke smiled. "It's been a long time, but I guess I do feel at home in this seat. It brings back a lot of memories, but most of them aren't good."

Meagan laughed as she flicked the power switch past the detent marked cassette and aligned it with the radio demarcation. The single speaker emitted a harsh static buzz. "Unless he had it tuned to static for white noise, whatever station it was set to is no longer broadcasting." She quickly spun the tuning knob and the orange indicator rapidly traveled down the frequency numbers to eighty-seven. She slowly drew her finger across the frequency selector again, this time in the opposite direction. The indicator climbed up the frequencies. The speaker weakly emitted the familiar tune of a top forty hit. The sound clarified and she stopped. "Here's one that's still broadcasting."

"No, that's an iPod station out of Atlanta."

"An iPod station?" she asked, arching her eyebrows.

"That's what I call them. It's a station where they have a big playlist on a computer and put it on random. The computer just plays songs. It doesn't have to have anybody there to keep it going."

"Got it," she said as she continued through the frequency range. She stopped at several more stations long enough to see if there was a DJ. They all seemed to be pre-recorded or playing from a random playlist.

"It was a good idea anyway," Zeke said. "I guess we're not going to be getting any information after all."

"Not so fast, we still have the AM stations." She flicked a selector from FM to AM and started backwards through the range. "We have a better chance of finding something here than on FM," she said, the hope in her voice being contagious.

"Nobody listens to AM radio. Why would we have a better chance?" Zeke questioned.

"Two reasons. First, AM stations tend to be more of the small mom and pop type of operation. They fill in unique niches. I would imagine that type of operation would be more likely to keep broadcasting. If you're working for a big corporation when all this breaks loose, you're not going to stick around. If you're working at the station you have poured your life into, you won't be so quick to abandon it.

"Secondly, AM radio waves are lower frequency transmissions. They bounce off the ionosphere and are reflected back down to earth long distances from where they were broadcast: in effect, they can get around the curvature of the earth. FM signals are higher frequency. They pass right through the ionosphere without being reflected. They're good for line of sight only."

"How in the world do you know about that?" Zeke asked.

"Same as you, Chemistry Boy. I have a physics minor. I learned it in college." Halfway through the frequencies, a voice came in through loud static. Meagan moved the antenna around and it disappeared.

"I would undo whatever you just did," Zeke advised.

"Thank you, Captain Obvious," she retorted quickly as she moved the antenna back to its initial orientation. The signal returned. It wasn't clear, but it was understandable. More importantly, it was a live broadcast. They listened for an hour straight to what was mostly old news, rumor, and hearsay. A phone rang in the studio and the commentator apologized, stating he was expecting a call from his son and had to take it, but would continue with more information after the call.

"He doesn't have anything to say anyway," Zeke said in frustration. He continued to sit and listen to the one sided phone conversation coming through the radio. Zeke removed his own phone from his pocket and looked at it.

It still showed no reception. "The cell network is still down," he said in frustration. Finally, he stood and said, "I'm going to bed."

As he stood, the commentator returned. "Sorry about that, folks. I did glean some news from my son, who is stationed at Hill Air Force Base in Utah. The military has reversed its policy of enforcing the President's flight ban. There is no point anymore. The infection has taken hold of the entire country. I'm going to call it a night. Tune in tomorrow for continued updates. Good night and God Bless." The signal turned to static.

"Did you hear that? The flight ban has been lifted. This changes everything," Zeke said excitedly.

Chapter 28

The first hints of the predawn light gently entered the sick room through the narrow windows at the top of the east wall, slowly dragging Zeke out of a deep sleep. His eyes opened, but his body wasn't yet ready to pull itself out of bed and start the day. He looked across the room to where Meagan was still sleeping, barely visible in the dim light. Although the room was scarcely illuminated, he could see a semi smile creeping across her face as something or someone in her imagined world brought happiness to her life that was becoming harder to find in the world of harsh reality she would shortly be returning to.

As he watched her in her secret moment of joy, he realized that over the past two days, she had been the sole source of joy and happiness in his own life. He didn't know if it was because she was the only person in his life at a time when he truly needed companionship, or if she truly was a person he was compatible with. They had worked together for nearly a year. At least they had worked for the same company. They had been acquaintances, nothing more. They hadn't really interacted. In the new world that had been thrust upon them, maybe compatibility was simply a man and woman with beating hearts. Maybe the lack of uninfected people left to choose from would change people's views of relationship suitability.

He found her physically attractive and since they had escaped from Mildred and Lester's home, he found himself becoming attracted to her as a person as well. As he pondered his future with her, Meagan's eyes slowly opened and came to rest on where he lay in his own bed.

"Were you watching me sleep?"

He nodded his head in affirmation.

"That's a little creepy, don't you think?" she asked, a mischievous smile forming at the corners of her mouth.

"It isn't like there was anything else to do. It's still too dark to see much and I didn't want to turn on any lights and draw the infected away from the entrance."

As the sun approached the horizon, the light entering the window changed hue. The white walls in the sick room transformed to a light shade of peach. Neither Zeke nor Meagan spoke. Both lay in silence, not wanting to disturb the peacefulness of the morning, a peacefulness they both knew was shortly coming to an end. In a matter of hours, they would be fleeing from their bulwark of safety, running headlong into the danger lurking just passed the heavy doors on the front of the building.

Finally Zeke sat up, swung his legs over the edge of his bed, put his feet in his shoes, and tied the laces. Meagan watched him and then sat up herself. She raised her arms above her head and moaned as she stretched the night's stiffness from her body. "What's the plan?" she asked.

"I was thinking about running down the road to the diner and getting a cup of coffee and a plate of eggs, bacon and pancakes, but I'm open for suggestions."

"Really?" she said, scrunching her forehead up. "Breakfast does sound pretty inviting, now that you mention it. Do you think G. Howe would mind if we cooked up some more of his steaks?" They had jokingly agreed two nights before to leave IOUs for G. Howe, the unknown provider of the steaks they had been plowing through every night. The chances were highly unlikely that he would ever come looking for his meat stash, so they hadn't felt guilty eating it.

"We ought to cook up some of those eggs too. I can't imagine the power is going to last much longer. It would be a shame for all that food to go to waste. Besides, it might be a long time before we have a chance to eat this well again," Zeke added, his mouth already beginning to water at the thought of steak and eggs.

After a leisurely breakfast, Meagan leaned back in her chair and asked, "When do I get to see the product of your chemistry genius in action?"

"First of all, I'm not a chemistry genius. I mostly got B's except for when I got the occasional C. Secondly, I don't think you want to be around when it happens. I've never set this much off before. I'm hoping that it goes off when I want it to and not before. And third, we're not quite ready. We need to build an apparatus to make sure we get the maximum benefit from what we have. I saw a pile of lumber in the maintenance shop. I need to build a framework to hang the bomb from. We also need a big container to fill with all the metal we can find. I'm sure the maintenance shop has a good supply of screws and nails. That stuff will make great shrapnel."

"I'll trust you on that one." Meagan was noticeably uncomfortable with the whole idea of setting off the homemade bomb, especially with Zeke's insinuations regarding its safety, or lack thereof.

An hour later, they had hauled a large pile of supplies up

to the roof. Zeke began nailing two by fours together. When he was done, he had constructed a twenty four foot tall, U shaped framework. Meagan, who had been inside the building trying to find items on a wish list Zeke had put together, returned to the rooftop and studied his clumsy looking contrivance.

"What exactly am I looking at?" she questioned, obviously unimpressed with both the crudeness of the workmanship as well as the object itself.

"Assuming you were able to locate some rope, we're going to use this to suspend the bomb over the center of the horde in order to increase its lethal radius. Give me a hand and help me get it in position."

After he explained how he wanted to position it, the two of them slowly lowered the framework over the side of the roof. The legs of the upside down U bracketed either side of the entrance to the building. When the legs were lowered to the ground, the infected showed no interest in the pine boards. However, they continued to show great interest in Zeke and Meagan.

When Zeke had first climbed onto the roof that morning, the number of infected near the building had shrunk to about fifty. During the night, many had lost interest and wondered away. Of those that had stayed, only a handful had remained near the door. Most had spread out around the parking lot and school grounds and were milling about aimlessly. Zeke walked to the edge of the roof and surveyed the population below. When he began his construction project, he intentionally worked near the edge of the roof, assuring he was in plain view. His presence alone quickly garnered the attention of the milling mob below. At first soft moans made their way up to his ears as individuals looked up and saw him. He was an object of curiosity. Then, as neurotransmitters began diffusing across synapses in still intact areas of the brains below, old memories were retrieved and connections were made in defunct minds. He moved from being on object of curiosity to an object of food. He became a means of satisfying the gnawing hunger in the stomachs of each infected below. Although they likely didn't feel pain from the hunger, the feeling fueled an instinctual urge within them to feed. Some made the connection instantly upon seeing him. Others took several seconds, but eventually even the most damaged brains figured it out.

Curious moans turned to excited shrieks which drew nearby infected. The size of the mob steadily grew. Hungry shrieks turned to howls of frustration with the realization that a newly discovered meal was out of reach. The frustration rapidly turned to screams of rage. The increasing volume echoed off the walls of the brick building. The arrival of each individual body added to the volume of the ruckus, which caused the sound to carry farther and farther. The disturbance soon became loud enough to draw infected from all over town.

Although Zeke was unaware, the feeding cries had such a powerful attraction that individuals locked in their houses became agitated and started breaking through windows and cheaply made doors in order to get to the source of the commotion. The size of the crowd quickly grew to about two hundred, with more joining the fracas every minute.

With the legs of the upside down U on the ground, the top of it was several feet above the roof line. Using a length of rope Meagan had found in the maintenance shop, Zeke suspended an orange five-gallon bucket a foot below the top of the U. The seventy pounds of screws, nails, bolts, nuts, and washers bowed the two by four under their weight. Near the top of the mixture of assorted hardware, Zeke gently placed a plastic container full of a white powder. A closer examination would have revealed it to be a crystalline substance that resembled sugar. A thin gauge wire protruded through the plastic lid of the container in two places. Inside the container, the wire dipped into the white powder, forming a U. Two rolls of a much heavier gauge wire had been soldered to either end of the U before it was placed in the powder and the heavy wire had been run across the roof, down the hall, and into the maintenance shop where the ends lay on the concrete floor beside a new car battery.

As Meagan watched curiously, Zeke tied a long piece of rope to the top of the lumber frame and stretched the rope ten feet back to the base of an air conditioning unit, making a loop around the square metal housing with several feet of slack between the unit and the wooden frame. The frame stood up straight with the legs sitting on the ground flush against the wall of the building. Zeke pushed the frame outward, away from the building, while keeping tension on the rope. As the frame leaned away from the wall, the force of its pull on the rope increased. Zeke let the rope slowly slide through his hands until it was taut between the frame and the air conditioning unit. The top of the frame leaned a couple feet from the wall with the bucket suspended a foot below.

Zeke walked back to the AC unit, took the end of the rope from Meagan, and slowly let it slide through his hands. The friction of the loop around the AC unit allowed him to maintain control as the wood frame leaned further from the

THE FLIGHT

building, gaining more leverage and exerting a greater pull on the rope. Eventually the frame was at a forty-five degree angle between the side of the building and the ground, the rope suspending the top of the frame twelve feet above the mob of infected. The bucket of potential shrapnel surrounding the bowl of homemade explosives swung back and forth in the light breeze ten feet above their heads.

A search of the main office turned up the master list for the combinations to every locker in the hall. While Zeke was building the frame from which to hang his improvised explosive device, Meagan had searched the lockers, coming up with several backpacks which she filled with drinks and candy bars from the vending machines in the teachers' room. She loaded the packs into the truck. While she had been gathering bolts, screws, nails, nuts, and washers for the IED, she came across an oak table that was being refinished in the maintenance shop. The legs had been removed and lay on a workbench. She picked one up to replace the club she had set down beside the painting supplies when they climbed the ladder two days ago.

Zeke and Meagan moved to the edge, looking down at the horde below. It was pressed up tight against the wall and door to the building.

"Is the truck ready?" he asked. He already knew the answer as he had helped load it, but he was nervous. Once they left the ledge, the group might begin to spread out again. Right now they were smashed together, one on top of the next like a pile of pancakes in a vacuum-sealed bag. They couldn't pack in any tighter, and Zeke wanted them to stay like that in order for the bomb to achieve its maximum effect.

"The truck's loaded," she answered patiently. "I have two backpacks of food and two backpacks of drinks on the front seat. I also packed the ax you found. I think we're ready."

"The bolt cutters are still in the truck?" he asked, confirming what he already knew to be true. He was the one who carefully placed the massive set of cutters on the front seat. They were an integral part of his plan to flee to California.

"They're still resting on the middle of the front seat where you put them. Everything's ready," she said reassuringly. It was obvious that he was getting nervous about leaving. They were about to flee from what had become a bastion of security into the terror and uncertainty that awaited outside. Zeke was only too familiar with the horrors they would face when they left the school.

"Okay then," Zeke said. "I'll stay here for a minute to keep their attention. Head to the shop and start the truck. I'll be right behind you."

Meagan hurried across the rooftop and disappeared through the hole in the roof. Zeke banged on the roof with a hammer, working the infected into a mad frenzy. Sixty seconds slowly ticked by. He ran to the hole in the roof and dropped the hammer to the floor below and then carefully lowered himself down until his foot tentatively found the first rung of the ladder. So far so good. He checked his watch. Fifteen seconds had passed since he left the edge of the roof. His feet pounded down the hall, each step echoing off the walls. As he neared the open door into the shop, the smell of exhaust began to burn the back of his throat. It was a good sign. It meant the engine was running, indicating the truck was ready.

He followed the twin lines of blue insulated wire into the shop. They ended beside a car battery two feet from the open driver side of the truck.

"Here goes nothing," he shouted as he picked up the ends of the two wires and touched the stripped end of one wire to the positive terminal of the battery and the other to the negative terminal. The idea was that the high resistance of the small gauge, U shaped wire in the bowl of explosives would cause the wire to heat up red hot. The super-heated wire in contact with the explosives should be enough to start breaking the weak bonds in the TATP and set off the chain reaction.

Nothing happened.

Meagan spoke, "Did it go..." The building shook and the windows rattled as a deep boom exploded through the hallway. Dust shook from the rafters overhead and wisps of insulation from the ceiling floated to the floor. Zeke's ears rang sonorously, and he was startled by the ferocity of the explosion. It was far bigger than any he had set off in the past.

He quickly overcame his surprise, ran to the rollup door, pushed the green button on the electric opener on the side of the wall, and sprinted for the truck as the monstrous door slowly clinked its way open. Once he could see light through the rearview mirror, he dropped the transmission into reverse. The tires chirped on the smooth epoxy coating the concrete floor as he gunned the engine. The truck shot from the bay into the exposed insecurity of the outside world. He looked over his left shoulder as he cranked the wheel in that direction. There were no infected behind them or in front of them. Once clear of the shop, he shifted to drive and romped on the gas.

"Aren't you going to close to garage door?"

"No. We don't have the time and if we need to retreat back to the school, that's the only way in." The tires squealed as he accelerated down the asphalt drive that ran parallel to the hallway in the building. The engine roared as huge quantities of gasoline were injected into each cylinder.

As the truck barreled past the front of the building, Zeke looked to his left, examining the outcome of his work. The doors to the building were gone, having been blown into the hallway from the force of the explosion, and the ground around the entrance was a writhing mass of bodies.

It had worked. The explosion had killed the majority of the horde. The plastic bowl full of TATP was instantaneously converted to ozone and other gasses. The volume the newly formed gasses occupied was orders of magnitude greater than the area the solid explosive had taken up. As the chemical reaction changed the solid crystals into gasses, the gasses expanded outward in all directions at supersonic speeds. The mass of nails, screws, bolts, nuts and washers that surrounded the bowl of explosives were also hurtled away from the explosion at nearly the same velocity. Each metallic object in the bucket was turned into a lethal projectile and was driven away from the blast in a high velocity cloud of death. The missiles that were driven into infected brains brought about instant death. The force of the explosion, as well as the force of the impact between projectiles and flesh, severed limbs and left bloody, broken bodies crawling over each other like a knot of worms. Blood painted the area surrounding the entrance a sea of crimson. One hundred feet away, splotches of blood and severed limbs marked the sidewalk, grass, and parking lot like the canvas of a demented abstract painter.

Howls and shrieks from the infected overshadowed the roar of the still accelerating engine. Whether the outcry of the mangled bodies was from pain or from fury at the inability to get to the passing truck didn't really matter.

A handful of infected that had been on the periphery of the crush of bodies had been shielded from the blast and the hail of projectiles. These ran at the truck, their faces contorted in rage, hunger, or agony.

Meagan stared at the scene of carnage after they turned onto the street, her mouth agape, shocked at the brutality of the explosion. Unable to tear her eyes away from the scene of destruction, she continued looking over her shoulder as the school shrank away behind the truck.

For the first mile or so, the streets were abandoned, showing no signs of life. Every infected within earshot of the school had been irresistibly drawn to the commotion preceding the explosion. Whether they sought food or were simply attracted to noise, the effect was the same: they could not resist the impulse that drove them to the source of the maelstrom about to be unleashed.

Houses along the street showed broken out windows and broken down doors, signs that trapped infected had battered their way out of their former homes only to be torn apart outside the school. Faces in intact homes peered out enviously as the truck sped past, leaving the local chaos and death behind, presumably headed to a safer environment. For each set of faces peering out, there was a car in front of the house or in a garage. All of them could have fled, but because of fear, or a lack of a better place to ride out the apocalypse, they refused to leave the perceived safety of their homes.

As distance from the school increased, so did the number of bodies ambling aimlessly in the road. The event replayed repeatedly. A body would turn its head toward the sound of the approaching pickup. Seconds would pass before jumbled memories came together in rotted brains and recognition briefly spread across a blank face. Recognition rapidly turned to fury and the individual or group would charge the truck. Time after time, Zeke would swerve at the last second, dodging the charging bodies obstructing his path.

As the truck swerved, the infected invariably lunged at the passing vehicle. A head slammed into the windshield, spreading a web of cracks radiating outward across the passenger side. Another hit the driver side mirror, exploding the plastic housing into a thousand pieces and shattering the glass as the assembly pivoted inward with such force that it hit the side window, sending a cascade of broken glass showering in on Zeke.

"Zeke!" Meagan exclaimed several miles from the school. "We're going the wrong way. California is the other direction."

Further from town, the infected finally disappeared from the road. Zeke turned to Meagan. "The plan has changed. I think I have a better route home, but we can't start from here. We have to back track a little to get to the starting point."

Chapter 29

Twenty minutes later, Zeke stopped in front of a closed gate barring entrance to the West Georgia Regional Airport. "This is as far as we drive," he said as he pulled the truck into the grass strip at the side of the entrance to the airport and turned off the engine.

"Let's get over that fence," he said, looking down the road behind them. They had passed three infected a mile back. When he last saw the group in the mirror, they were still chasing the truck. The group hadn't come into view yet, but Zeke knew it was only a matter of time before they did.

He and Meagan hurriedly threw bags and tools over the fence. Last was a red fire ax he had liberated from the wall in the shop. A shriek down the road hurried him as he double checked the truck, making sure nothing had been overlooked. He shut the door and looked down the road again, catching a glimpse of the three bodies rushing toward them.

The mile they had sprinted didn't seem to have slowed them at all. Their energy seemed limitless.

"We have to get over that fence," he admonished Meagan, who was watching with a mixture of fascination and fear as the group closed to a quarter mile.

Zeke bent over and interlaced his fingers, holding them

between his knees to give her a boost. Meagan looked at him with a raised eyebrows and a smirk before proceeding to lithely scale the fence without his assistance.

"Come on, Flyboy. I need you on this side of the fence. I don't know how to drive an airplane."

Zeke awkwardly pulled himself over the fence in a spectacle that was completely devoid of the grace and finesse Meagan had demonstrated. By the time he was on the other side, Meagan had already hung a strap from each of the backpacks of food over one of her shoulders and picked up her oak club and small canvas tool bag. "Where's your plane?" she inquired.

Zeke shrugged as he quickly shouldered the two bags of drinks and picked up the bolt cutters and ax. "I don't actually have a plane. We're going to have to borrow one. We're looking for something that's fast and has a full tank of gas."

Carrying their loads of gear, they quickly ran toward a long hanger ahead. Along the ramp in front of the hanger, a dozen planes were lined up facing the road. Many were derelicts far past their prime, the airworthiness of several was questionable. None were what he was looking for. He briefly eyed several old, underpowered twins. Their increased payload and interior space didn't make up for their lumbering slow speeds and increased fuel burn. In theory, the extra engine was supposed to take the plane to safety if one engine failed. In reality, the extra engine doubled the chances of a catastrophic engine failure. For these smaller twins, even when brand new, the second engine barely had the power to maintain altitude. On the aged specimens of aeronautical history sitting on the ramp before them, the second engine would have just enough

THE FLIGHT

power to carry them to the scene of an airplane crash.

Bolt cutters in hand, Zeke approached the first hanger door. With little effort he severed the shank of the lock securing the door. He pushed the door open, revealing a sleek composite bodied airplane painted in a red, white, and blue paint scheme. A large, highly polished exhaust pipe came out either side of the cowling. Without bothering to shut the door, he hurried to the next.

Meagan peeked in after he moved on. "That one looked nice. Why can't we take it?" she asked, disappointed in passing on what was obviously a luxury craft.

"It would be perfect for somebody else," he said, his face turning red in embarrassment.

"Why wouldn't it be perfect for us?" she asked in confusion.

"It has a turbine engine. The shop I worked in during college only worked on piston powered engines and I have only flown piston powered airplanes," he said as his bolt cutters crushed through another lock. "I don't know how to start it."

Meagan futilely attempted to stifle a laugh. "That's too bad because I really liked that one."

Zeke wasn't satisfied with the slow, short range Cessna 152 and continued to the end of the building, not finding what he was looking for in any of the bays.

The three ghouls had reached the gate and were throwing themselves against it noisily. The fencing rattled and the assaulting body bounced off with each failed attempt to breach the chain link barrier.

Zeke hurried to the other side of the hanger and began clipping his way through the locks down the building and then back up the building across the way.

"Zeke, I think you're being too picky. Can't we just take one of these and go?"

"None of these will make it across the country without multiple stops. Each time we have to land and refuel, we are exposing ourselves to a lot of risk. The power may be down and we might not be able to get any fuel. The airport might be overrun with infected. We might run into somebody we don't want to meet. I'm looking for something that can make it with only one stop."

He pushed another giant sliding door to the side, revealing a small, low wing aircraft. A large bubble canopy sat over two, side by side seats in a tight cockpit. A shiny chrome spinner rested at the front of a white, three bladed propeller with red tips. Purple stripes swirled down the white fuselage. The aircraft sat on three tiny, retractable wheels. It was the sky's equivalent of a Ferrari. "This is it!" he blurted out excitedly as he passed through the narrow opening in the nine foot tall rolling doors. "A Lancair 360! Get in here!"

Meagan followed him into the hanger and he rolled the door closed behind her. Translucent plastic roofing panels allowed light to shine into the hanger.

Zeke walked around the wing and pushed the canopy forward over the engine, opening the cockpit. "Stow your gear behind the seat." He looked at the instrument panel and added, "There's no key. We have a little work to do before we can leave." He dropped his two bags into the modest cargo space behind the seat and quickly removed the fuel caps from each wing and one more behind the engine. After inspecting each of the three fuel bays, he announced, "She's topped off with fuel."

Zeke pulled a screw driver from the canvas bag and

began undoing the fasteners that held the cowling over the engine. With access to the motor, he disconnected a wire from two metal boxes on top of it.

"What are you doing?" Meagan asked

"I'm disconnecting the magneto P leads," he said. "Airplanes are different from cars. When you turn the key to the on position, you aren't activating the starter; you're breaking the ground connection to the magnetos which are either of these boxes on top of the engine. The magnetos produce the electric impulses that arc across the ends of the spark plugs. The magneto can't produce a spark when it's grounded which is why we disconnected the P leads or the grounding wires. When we undo the ground wires, it enables the engine to run without the key. There's a separate button you push to activate the starter," he added as he put the cowl back over the engine.

"That's it? You don't have to do anything else?" she asked, surprised at how easy it was to steal an airplane.

"That's it. If you redo all these fasteners, I'll see if I can plan our trip real quick."

Zeke climbed into the cockpit and sat in the left seat. He clicked two red rocker switches up and a relay closed with a *pop*. A whirring began behind the instrument panel as the gyros spun up. Zeke began pushing buttons on the GPS unit in the panel. "How does Syracuse, Kansas sound?" he asked Meagan as he leaned his head out of the cockpit.

"I've never heard of it before, but it sounds good to me."

With the course programmed into the GPS, Zeke clicked the master switch down, cutting off battery power to the plane. The whine of the gyros slowed as they spun down.

Zeke examined the Cam-Lock fasteners as Meagan twisted the last one into place. "You're a natural. If you get tired of working at the investment firm, I'm sure you could get a job working on planes."

"Thanks. It's good to know I have options to fall back on if this doesn't work out for me," she replied sarcastically.

Zeke put his weight behind the door as he started rolling it open. A widening crack appeared, shooting a splinter of light across the hanger floor. A long shadow appeared in the bright column on the floor. Zeke turned and saw an arm reaching through the opening. An angry scream pushed into the hanger from behind the arm. Zeke stopped the door before it opened wide enough for the body attached to the arm to gain entrance.

A *crash* echoed through the hanger as something smashed into the metal siding that covered the door. "Grab me the ax!" Zeke screamed.

Meagan dove into the plane, and dug through the luggage in the back. She unzipped a pocket on the side of the food bag and removed a paper face mask she found in the sick room back at the school. She pulled the fire ax from beneath the bag and scurried to the crack between the wall and the rolling door as she fitted the mask over her mouth and nose. The frustrated arm continued to reach through the gap, fingers opening and closing. A face crammed up to the gap, unable to fit through.

"Roll it open a couple more inches," Meagan suggested apprehensively.

"It'll let him in," Zeke countered, vehemently opposed to the idea.

"No, he's too fat," she disagreed. "Another couple inches and I can split his head."

"Are you sure?"

"Yeah, I'm sure," she said, hoping she was right.

Zeke slowly pushed the door. The head pushed its way into the opening, teeth clacking loudly as they sought Meagan's skin in vain. The head hissed loudly in frustration. Outside, two separate howls echoed off the metal hangers.

"Push it closed," she shouted.

Zeke obeyed without questioning, rolling the door back the other way. It moved a couple inches before it stopped, the thick neck of the encroaching body blocking the way. Meagan lifted the ax over her head, closed her eyes and brought it down in a crashing blow on the back of the intruder's skull. The ax blade sank three inches into the skull. The head and arm slid down the face of the wall and door, collapsing to the floor. A second arm reached for Meagan as she struggled to free the ax from the infected's cranium. It was tightly wedged in and she couldn't free it regardless of how hard she pulled. Finally, she put her foot on the head and leaned back, pulling as hard as she could, leveraging the ax up and down. It suddenly wrenched free. She was leaning back so far she couldn't keep her balance when the ax was freed and she fell backwards, landing hard on the floor.

She quickly stood, picked up the ax, and buried it in the second head poking through the slender opening. This time she kept her eyes open, but couldn't keep a grimace from spreading across her face as she completed the gruesome task of bashing in the man's head.

The second body collapsed on top of the first only to be

replaced by the head of the third infected, its teeth *clacking* violently. Again, the second skull held the ax fast in place. Careful to stay clear of the groping arm and *clicking* teeth, Meagan once again freed the ax and, this time, was able to maintain her footing. She swung again, crushing the third head with the blunt end of the ax. The body crumpled to the ground, blood from its mangled head adding to the rapidly growing scarlet pool forming around the dead trio.

"I think it's clear now," she hollered to Zeke.

"Then get in the plane."

She crawled over the left wing and sat in the left seat. Zeke put his weight behind the door and it rolled open. "Unless you're planning on flying, get in the other seat," he shouted as the door slammed against the stop at the end of its travel. With the doors open, Zeke ran across the hanger, leaped onto the wing, wedged himself into the seat Meagan had just vacated, pulled the canopy closed, and showed Meagan how to fasten the latches on her side to secure the canopy.

"Fuel selector – check, brakes – check, beacon –we'll skip that one, circuit breakers – check, master on – check, mixture rich – check, prime engine – check."

"Zeke! Problem!"

Zeke halted his pre-start up checklist and looked out the cockpit to where Meagan pointed. A lone man stood in the center of the hanger door. His grizzled face had a huge, bloody sore below his ear as if a bite had been torn from it. He looked dumbly into the hanger, sensing something, but not sure what it was. The sun reflecting off the canopy blinded him to what was beyond the thin Plexiglas. The hum of the electric fuel pump held his gaze as his mind feebly attempted to determine what it meant.

THE FLIGHT

"We'll forgo the checklist in favor of an expedited departure." Zeke pulled the throttle back and pushed in the silver starter button at the bottom left of the panel. The prop began rotating and the engine sputtered intermittently as the blades arced around.

The sound of the spinning prop and engine grabbed the man's attention. He was drawn to the sound and motion like a moth to a flame. He ran forward as the engine caught and accelerated the prop momentarily before it coughed again, spitting black exhaust from the pipes sticking out the bottom of the cowling. The prop was spinning fast enough that it had disappeared in a rotating blur. A hand reached for the engine cowl, instinctively drawn to the sound. The rapidly spinning propeller severed the arm. Even if the man's brain was capable of realizing what was happening, he couldn't have stopped his forward motion fast enough. His body collided with the propeller. The blade crashed into the top of his skull, slicing his face from his head. The force of the spinning blade threw his body to the side. The engine caught and revved loudly. Zeke quickly reduced the throttle and let his feet off the brake pedals.

The plane rolled forward several feet and suddenly jolted to an abrupt halt. He pushed the throttle knob forward dumping gas to the engine. The four cylinders roared, but the plane refused to budge.

"I think the body is in front of the right wheel. I'm going to have to shut it down and move him."

"You don't have time," Meagan reported, pointing to an approaching group of five more men and a woman.

"Hang on!" Zeke firewalled the throttle. Torque from the engine dipped the left wing toward the ground. The left side of the plane began to pivot slowly around the blocked right wheel. Zeke applied the left brake to stop the rotation. The right wing lurched upward as the thrust of the propeller pulled the small wheel over the corpse.

The huge volume of air being pushed rearward by the propeller picked up every piece of dirt and debris from the unkempt floor. The air and dirt hit the back wall, rising up toward the ceiling where the airflow pushed it forward out of the cavernous opening. The blinding dust cloud obscured the approaching infected as well as the parallel set of hangers seventy feet across the taxiway. As the plane shot into the open, Zeke pulled the throttle back and stomped on the left brake pedal. The nose wheel pivoted and the plane turned to the left. When he estimated he had turned through ninety degrees, he applied the right brake to straighten it out and align with the taxiway between the two hangers.

The aircraft pulled out of the dust cloud and the bodies emerged just in front of the plane. Zeke pulled the throttle back to idle, slowing the propeller before it mowed a path through the mob of people. Meagan covered her head with her hands as blood splattered down the right side of the plane, partially obscuring the windshield on her side. Several bodies outside of the propeller's radius were struck by the wing. Two disappeared beneath the plane. The third was folded over, his torso draped across the wing top while his legs trailed below. He reached angrily toward the cockpit. Zeke increased the throttle. In response, the speed the plane was taxiing increased. The forward motion held the body pinned to the leading edge of the wing.

This side of the airport had not been well maintained. Large sections of asphalt had cracked and dropped with the settling earth beneath, leaving two-inch gaps between sections. Zeke taxied at nearly fifteen miles per hour, a fast taxi even on a smooth taxiway, and the plane jolted and jostled as the wheels dropped to lower sections or bounded up raised sections.

The jostling bounced the infected man around like a ball of yarn batted by a playful kitten. Despite the bouncing and bumping, he continued to stay firmly affixed to the leading edge of the wing three feet away from the canopy. Zeke transitioned onto the main taxiway, which was well maintained. The recently paved black surface was as smooth as a freshly chipped piece of obsidian. There was no hope of bouncing the hitchhiking passenger off the wing.

In the half mile to the end of the runway, Zeke tried to finish as much of the pre-takeoff checklist as he could. A quarter mile from the runway threshold, he told Meagan to watch as he fastened the five point harness. Instead of a simple lap belt like the airlines, this plane had straps that went over each shoulder in addition to a thick strap across the lap. It was typical of an aerobatic plane. Even inverted, the occupant was held firmly in his seat.

Meagan attempted to mimic his actions, but he went too fast and lost her. He looked over and saw her bewilderment. "No, this one goes last," he said.

"Got it," she said, threading the parts together and pulling the clasp down to lock the buckles of each strap in place.

The taxiway made a ninety degree turn to the runway. Rather than pulling back on the throttle, Zeke pushed it in further. When the front wheel of the plane aligned with the white dashed lines that designated the center of the runway, Zeke push the throttle all the way in. The light plane leapt forward as the propeller took huge bites of air, clawing its way down the runway. The man still clung to the wing, inching his way closer to the cockpit.

As the plane hurtled down the mile-long raceway, a figure ambled out of the grass and onto the runway two hundred and fifty yards away, eyeing the oncoming aircraft. Zeke watched the airspeed indicator as the white needle passed through sixty miles per hour. "If we hit her, this flight is over before it begins," Zeke murmured to himself more than to Meagan.

The distance between the woman and the plane rocketing down the runway closed at an alarmingly fast rate. At eighty miles an hour, Zeke pulled back on the stick, a mere hundred feet from the woman. The nose of the plane pitched skyward. The rest followed as it leapt into the air. The body draped over the left wing interfered with the air flowing over it and greatly reduced the lift it was creating. As soon as the wheels left the ground, the extra weight on the wing coupled with the reduced lift caused the left wing tip to dip dangerously close to the ground. The whole plane shuddered as it passed over the woman and the dangling nose wheel slammed into her face, knocking her dead on the asphalt runway. Zeke pushed the control stick to the right and leveled the drooping left wing. With the plane airborne and stable, he flipped a toggle switch that retracted the landing gear.

Even if the infected man wanted to let go of the wing, Zeke wasn't sure if the hundred mile per hour wind would permit him to wiggle free. Shortly after takeoff, at an altitude of fifteen hundred feet, Zeke told Meagan to hang on. He pulled back further on the stick and then pushed it to the left. The agile craft rolled rapidly. Zeke looked out the window at the left wing tip. As it approached eighty degrees of bank, he slowed the roll rate. The tip of the wing pointed straight toward the ground and the man slid down its length, plummeting to the earth's surface.

With the man clear of the wing, Zeke pushed the stick to the left again and the plane rolled upside down, and then continued rolling until it came right side up. Meagan screamed and then yelled, "That beats any rollercoaster!"

Chapter 30

After nearly five hours of flying over a patchwork quilt of fields ranging from various shades of green all the way to brown, Zeke announced they were nearly at their destination. They had crossed half the country at an altitude of ninety-five hundred feet, high enough that the details of towns, ranches, and small estates blended into obscurity.

Cars appeared as tiny dots parked along streets, in front of houses, and in parking lots. Occasionally one crawled along a road or highway below. Even at sixty miles an hour, a car was traveling a quarter of the speed they were and looked like a tiny insect slowly traversing a barren and featureless landscape.

Plumes of black smoke billowed from towns engulfed in raging flames. Some were set by looters, others by accident. Firemen who weren't infected had abandoned their stations. Even if they desired to put out the blazes, it was suicide; there were too many infected rampaging through the streets. Just like everybody else, the firemen had families who needed to be protected, wives and children who needed to be comforted. The only thing that would stop the fires was when the fuel was exhausted. With their homes and shelters destroyed, fleeing families had little chance of survival.

At nearly two miles above the chaos and struggles for

survival, Zeke and Meagan couldn't grasp the full scope of the fight for life taking place below. They understood the overall picture of what was happening because hours before, they had been in the midst of it. They understood the terror and hopelessness that unseen people below were fighting to overcome, but they could not see the specific plight of individual persons.

The world they were currently inhabiting was sterile and peaceful, although they were about to reenter the harsh and cruel macrocosm endured by the rest of humanity. As Zeke announced their imminent arrival, a sense of dread settled on both of them. Adrenaline caused a tingling in Zeke's stomach. Meagan's pulse quickened as her heart began to pound. Both silently wondered what they would find on the ground. There was no way to know if there would be fuel to continue their trek, or if the airport would be overrun by infected.

With both wing tanks empty and the auxiliary tank in the nose of the plane showing only a few gallons on the fuel meter, Zeke was more concerned with making it to the airport than he was over what they would find when they landed. He was unfamiliar with the particular quirks of the aircraft. He did know, however, that the FAA only required a fuel gauge to be accurate when it displayed full and empty. Between full and empty, they didn't care if it gave a true reading. He assumed the fuel gauge was reasonably accurate, but an inaccuracy of a gallon or two would mean the difference between landing safely at the airport or crashing somewhere short of their destination with a silent engine and a slowly windmilling propeller mocking their helpless state.

Rather than beginning a slow descent, Zeke maintained

his altitude, hoping to keep a margin of safety in case the gas gauge was off and they ran out of fuel. Although the thin wings would not provide a good glide ratio if the engine quit, the extra altitude provided a reassuring buffer which would enable them to glide at least twenty miles.

"The airport should be out there," he told Meagan as he pointed straight ahead. "It should be fifteen miles in front of us. If you see it, let me know." Several minutes later, Zeke spotted a narrow black ribbon at the north edge of a town. "There it is," he pointed. "We're going to come in high and circle down to make sure it's safe."

Zeke banked to the left as he crossed the middle of the runway. The orange windsock was pointed straight out, nearly perfectly aligned down runway three-one. More importantly, the runway was clear of obstructions and he couldn't see any infected near the airport.

His main concern with the airport was that it bordered the edge of the city. He was afraid the sound of the engine would bring every infected from the small town to the airport. Planning the trip back in Georgia, he hadn't realized the threat this posed. At this point, there wasn't enough fuel to try for a different airfield. They were committed regardless of what happened.

Zeke pushed the mixture and propeller control knobs all the way in. The RPM gauge inched up just short of red line. He pulled out the throttle knob, causing a drop on the manifold pressure gauge. When they had descended to five thousand feet, he leveled out again. The airspeed bled down to one hundred twenty miles an hour and he flicked the gear switch to the down position. Two of the three green lights next to the switch illuminated. The third light, which represented the nose gear, remained dark. Zeke tapped the unlit bulb with his finger. Nothing happened.

Meagan, sensing his apprehension, asked, "What's wrong?"

"These three lights represent the landing gear. When a wheel is down, a green light comes on. The light for the nose wheel isn't coming on."

"What does that mean?" she asked.

"It means the nose wheel isn't all the way down. It was probably damaged when we hit the woman on the runway at takeoff." He flipped the switch up and the lights went out. He flipped it back down and the nose light still failed to illuminate. "I'm going to perform some abrupt maneuvers and see if we can shake it down and get it to lock in place. Hang on," he said hopefully.

He pulled back on the control stick and the nose shot up. Meagan felt her entire body pulled into the seat. She instantly felt like she weighed seven hundred pounds. She tried to lift her arm, but it was too heavy and remained pinned to her thigh. Her vision began to darken around the periphery until she was left with a small sphere of sight directly in front of her face.

Without warning, Zeke pushed the nose forward. For an instant, Meagan felt her body lift lightly off the seat. For the first time in her life, she experienced the same feeling of weightlessness that is normally reserved for astronauts. She felt a strange sensation in her stomach as her organs lifted within her body, floating in her abdominal cavity. As Zeke pushed further forward, the plane began a dive. The curiously pleasant sensation suddenly became utterly unbearable. Her body was violently pulled away from her seat as the plane descended faster than the pull of gravity and literally left her behind. The only thing that kept her from flying through the canopy was the seatbelt harness fastened tightly over her shoulders and lap. Her vision turned red as the effects of negative gravity forced excess blood into her head and eyes. The intense pressure it caused in her head nearly drove her out of her mind.

Zeke pulled back on the stick once again, pitching the nose up and slamming her back into her seat. The G force pinned her arms back to her sides. With side pressure on the stick, the plane rolled violently and Meagan's head slammed into the side of the canopy. The ground and sky switched places as the plane rolled inverted. She lost all sense of orientation.

As the plane rolled upright again, Zeke pushed the stick over in the opposite direction. Meagan slammed into his shoulder as the plane rolled to the right, causing the horizon to spin wildly. Meagan's stomach became queasy. The remnants of her early morning breakfast threatened to violently reappear.

The sky returned to its proper location above them and Zeke pulled back on the stick. The nose of the plane pitched up, yet again. It kept rising until it was pointed at the noon sun, directly overhead. The plane climbed straight up, rapidly losing speed until it momentarily hung on the screaming propeller. Unable to hold itself in the thin air, the craft began falling back to earth, tail first. Zeke pushed the stick forward and air flowing backwards over the elevator caused the craft to pitch over, once again showing its belly to the sky. Then the nose pointed straight down and the altimeter, which had peaked at eight thousand feet, rapidly unwound, the needles spinning backwards as the plane rocketed toward the ground. Zeke pulled the throttle back as he tugged back on the stick.

Meagan was shoved into her seat as the force of gravity her body was subjected to increased six times above normal.

As the plane leveled out, Meagan began to heave. She tried to put her head between her legs, directing the vomit to the floor. For a second, she felt better, but the smell of her own puke quickly brought on another round of upheaval, this one even more violent than the first.

She turned behind the seat, looking for the bag of beverages to wash the bitter taste from her mouth. The cargo net over the baggage had kept it in place during the violent maneuvers, but she couldn't reach it while belted into her seat. There was no way she was going to undo her seatbelt harness after the violence Zeke had just subjected her to.

"Please tell me you fixed the landing gear," she begged. "That better not have been for nothing." Unfortunately, she already knew the answer because she could plainly see the top light was still dark.

"I'm sorry," Zeke answered. "It didn't work. We're going to have land the way we are. We don't have enough fuel to keep monkeying around, hoping for a miracle."

He positioned the plane parallel to right side of the runway and flew several miles past the end before beginning a gentle, banking turn that lined the plane up with the long black strip of asphalt. With the Lancair lined up on the runway centerline, he flipped the gear switch back up and the two green lights extinguished.

"What are you doing?" Meagan questioned in confusion. "Did you just put the landing gear up?"

"If we land with the nose wheel up and the main gear down, the nose will dig in and the plane will flip upside down. We'll probably die. With all the gear up, it will slide down the runway on its belly. It will ruin the plane, but we'll most likely be okay."

"I thought planes catch on fire when they crash," Meagan countered with concern. She had faced a myriad of horrible ways to die over the past few days. All of them were preferable to burning to death, strapped into a tiny midget of an aircraft. "I think I would rather jump out right now than risk burning to death."

Half a mile from the end of the runway, the engine began to sputter and cough. And then it died. Except for the soft whistle of air passing over the body of the powerless plane, the cockpit was ominously silent.

"Well," Zeke began, "running out of fuel isn't all bad. At least we won't burn after we crash."

Chapter 31

Without the engine, the plane immediately began to slow. Zeke pushed the nose down, trading altitude for airspeed. His attention was focused on the runway designator numbers three-one which were painted on the end of the runway. A quick glance at the altimeter showed he was passing through five hundred feet. He was holding his airspeed at ninety miles an hour, which he estimated was the best glide speed. It didn't look like they were going to make the end of the runway.

A fleeting thought ran through his head and he realized he needed to get the canopy unlatched before they hit the ground. Once the plane hit, he was afraid the latches may jam, leaving them stuck in the plane. He quickly undid the two buckles on his side that secured it.

"Should I undo mine too?" Meagan asked.

"Yeah, we want to get out of the plane as quickly as we can when it stops moving." She undid the front latch easily. The back latch took all the strength she could muster. The fast moving air flowing over the glass created an area of low pressure, causing the canopy to pull away from the plane and creating tension on the locking mechanism. With a grunt, she popped it open.

The canopy rose three inches, blasting them with hot air that rushed under the front edge. Zeke squinted in response. At three hundred feet above the ground, his eyes did a quick one hundred-eighty degree sweep of the airport. He caught movement coming from hangers on the south side of the field. A group of people were running toward the runway.

At five feet above the grass at the end of the runway, Zeke pulled back on the stick to stop the sink rate and bleed off more speed. The propeller hit the ground first. The carbon fiber blade flexed and then shattered. The belly hit the ground for a split second. The plane rose back into the air and hit again, this time gently setting down fifty feet from the end of the pavement. It slid across the grass and then jolted as it transitioned to the asphalt runway at seventy-five miles an hour. Meagan covered her ears, trying to block out the scraping sound. The noise set her nerves on edge, making her cringe. A handful of people ran onto the runway just ahead of them. The plane continued sliding, slowly scrubbing away speed as it left a trail of shredded material behind; some of it embedded in the asphalt and some of it floating up in the wind behind them.

Zeke estimated the plane was still doing close to sixty miles an hour, but, since the pitot tube had been ground off, the airspeed indicator gave no reading. The leading edge of the right wing smashed into the front girl's legs just above the ankles and flipped her at least ten feet in the air. Meagan watched in horror as her body cart wheeled through the air before it disappeared behind the plane. She landed headfirst on the asphalt behind the sliding Lancair.

The impact to the wing caused the plane to yaw slowly as it skidded down the runway. Two more infected, running side by side, were taken out by the left wingtip. The plane violently spun to the left like an out of control top, but maintained a straight track along the centerline of the runway, taking out the rest of the group before it came to a stop.

Before the plane had ground to a halt, Zeke had begun unbuckling his seat belt. The dust had not yet settled before he was pushing the canopy all the way forward and stepping onto the splintered wing. Three infected were hastily approaching from behind. Their clothes were torn and their skin bloody from being slammed onto the runway by the sliding, spinning plane.

"Grab the ax from behind the seat!" Zeke screamed as he pulled his pistol from his holster. He knew the sound of gunfire would draw ten times what he could kill with the limited number of bullets remaining in his magazines.

One hundred infected attacking five minutes from now was something he would deal with in five minutes. Right now, the only thing that mattered was the three infected hobbling toward him at speeds that would rival a high school hundred meter runner.

He knew better than to shoot when they were beyond his effective range, but panic overcame reason. He fired his first shot at fifty yards. He knew he couldn't make a head shot on a bouncing and bobbing head from that range. He shot anyway. The man's hobbling gait sprang his body up every several paces. The gunshot coincided with one of those springing strides. The aim had been good, but the head moved up six inches as the round exploded from the barrel. The bullet smashed into the man's upper chest, knocking him flat on his back. He quickly rose to his feet and resumed his blitz behind his two consorts. Zeke fired two more rounds in rapid succession. Both sailed harmlessly between the two leading assailants a mere twenty five yards away. Three more shots flew downrange. The last one smashed into the nose of one of the on-rushers, who tumbled to the ground when the impulses telling its feet to move stopped racing down its spine.

Zeke adjusted his aim to the right and fired another barrage. At ten feet he didn't think he could miss, but he did. Three bullets hit the man, but they all missed his head. Zeke dove to the side as the twenty-something year old man lunged for him. They both landed on the ground at the same time, eight feet apart. They got up in unison as if performing a synchronized dance. Zeke brought the pistol up and fired a double tap into the advancing fiend. His aim was true and the man dropped at his feet.

As he turned back to the last attacker, Meagan swung her table leg like it was the bottom of the ninth with two outs. She connected with a blow that would have knocked a fastball way out of the park. Without waiting to see if the man would get back up, she pummeled him repeatedly until she was convinced he wasn't going to move anymore.

Zeke dashed back to the plane and began pulling their supplies out. As he dug, Meagan yelled, "Hurry up, there are more coming!" He looked up and saw fifty or sixty infected ambling toward them at a fast walk. He was pretty sure the only thing drawing them to the plane at this point was curiosity. There had been a lot of noise and they were coming to investigate.

"They're between us and the hangers," Meagan whispered. The infected were emerging from a large group of hangers at the south end of the field. "We might be able to make it to that shop to the west if we run. It'll be close." She dropped the pack she had around her shoulder and crouched behind the plane, out of sight of the oncoming mob. "What do you think?"

He looked toward the maintenance shop two to three hundred yards to their west and then peeked over the top of the fuselage. They still hadn't been spotted. "It's the only option I can see. I'll be right behind you."

Meagan crouched, looking around the plane and then took off at a sprint, table leg in her right hand. Zeke followed behind with the ax in his hand and his pistol in the holster. Two hundred and fifty yards is a long way to sprint, especially when carrying a two pound club. The herd of infected a quarter mile away provided the proper motivation to keep their pace recklessly fast.

They hadn't covered ten steps before they were spotted, and the clamor that arose from the group was the first indication. A second later, the group engaged in an intercepting line of pursuit.

Meagan was fast, but Zeke easily could have passed her. He stayed on her heels for the first hundred yards. He suddenly realized there was no reason for the shop to be unlocked. If the door wasn't open, every second they had could mean the difference between life and a violent death. With that thought in mind, he poured on the speed, blowing passed Meagan.

Her first thought was that he was abandoning her and leaving her to fend for herself. She lengthened her strides, finding speed she didn't realize she had. She still couldn't keep up and he continued to pull away.

The front of the hanger was a huge bi-fold door which was closed tight and couldn't be opened from the outside. A regular door stood in the adjacent wall. Zeke arrived at the door ten paces ahead of Meagan. He latched onto the handle and turned his wrist. His hand twisted around the stationary stainless steel handle. It was locked. He hung his head in despair. There was nowhere else to go. If they couldn't get into the building, they would be torn apart in a handful of seconds.

"Maybe there's a door in the back," Meagan huffed as she sprinted passed him. As Zeke followed her around the back of the building, their hopes were renewed. On the back side of the building was a window covered with a metal mesh screwed to the siding to prevent people from breaking in. Another door stood ten feet beyond the window.

Meagan beat him to the door. His spirits soared when she pushed into the door with her shoulder and it swung open. The interior of the shop was completely dark. The outside window faced into an office and did not provide any illumination into the cavernous work space. Zeke stepped into the rectangular strip of light pouring through the doorway. Unsure of what was in the dark recesses of the building, he was hesitant to close the door and plunge the building back into blackness.

Gravel crunched under fifty sets of running feet around the corner of the shop. The group had mostly fallen silent when Zeke and Meagan disappeared from sight. The crunching footfalls turned the corner to the back of the shop. With no other choice, Zeke slammed the door closed, his fingers fumbling for the lock in complete darkness.

"Zeke!" Meagan called from several feet away.

"I'm here," he whispered back, not wanting to further incite the bodies banging against the door. "I'm looking for the lights." He continued feeling his way along the wall until he found a bank of switches. He flicked them up one at a time and was greeted with a pop from the ceiling as the electricity energized each high voltage ballast connected to the lights.

Chapter 32

The interior of the shop began to illuminate as the lights warmed up. The floor was crammed full of planes, most of them appearing to be in various stages of maintenance or inspection. A low wing Piper in the corner was missing the engine. Other planes had inspection panels hanging by a single screw. All were old and in fair to poor condition. There was one exception. Parked in front of the bi-fold door was a Cessna twin engine painted white with a pair of red stripes swirling their way down the side of the fuselage like twin ribbons flowing in the breeze.

Zeke crossed the hanger, irresistibly drawn to the aircraft. It was an immaculately kept 421C Golden Eagle, the flagship of Cessna's line up from the late 70's and early 80's. The side door was down, the stair extending to a foot above the floor.

Zeke climbed the stair into the passenger compartment and scooted down the narrow isle between seats. Pushing aside the curtain that separated the cockpit from the cabin, he climbed into the passenger seat and *clicked* on the master switch. The gyros whined as they spun up in the instrument panel. He looked to the fuel gauges. Both rested squarely on empty.

Meagan stuck her head into the cockpit, looking over Zeke's shoulder. "Let me guess, you don't know how to start this one, either?" she mocked jokingly.

"Actually, I do know how to start this one. I have quite a bit of time flying in this model. The guy I worked for in college had one of these he used for charter flights. Several of the companies he flew for had corporate policies that required a copilot. I had a multiengine rating and got a lot of right seat time. Sometimes he let me fly from the left seat. It's been several years, but I think I can remember how to get the engines turning."

Meagan's face lit up. "So we have a ride out of here?" she asked enthusiastically. She looked around at the cockpit and back to the cabin behind. It was a far cry from the tight confines of the tiny shoe box they were crammed into for the first five hours of the trip. The instrument panel had several high tech LCD screens. It looked modern, and it inspired confidence. The cabin was wrapped in soft grey leather and rich wood paneling. The seats were plush and roomy.

"I could fly it, but according to the gauges, the fuel tanks are completely empty." Zeke shook his head sadly. "There's no way we can get to the fuel pumps outside without attracting too much unwanted attention. I'm afraid we're stuck."

Although dejected, Meagan refused to give up. "What about the other planes in here? Could you fly one of them?"

The hanger lights had warmed up to full brightness. Zeke looked around the hanger at the dozen or so smaller planes stacked into the hanger. "Yeah, I could fly any of these, but before we could takeoff, we would have to get the plane out of the hanger. This beast is blocking the way so we would have to move it first," he said, patting the wingtip as he walked around the twin. "Depending on which one we took, we might have to move four or five others to get it out. It would be a pretty risky venture. The big door is going to make a lot of noise when it starts to open and it doesn't open very fast."

As he walked around the front of the white twin engine, he picked up a clipboard resting on the wing. It was an inspection "squawk" sheet the mechanics used to log the progress of their maintenance. He looked over the one entry on the sheet. "That explains why there isn't any fuel in it. They just resealed the fuel selector valve. You have to drain the gas to get the valve out. It looks like the repair is done, it just needs fuel."

"What do they do with the fuel when they drain it out?" Meagan asked.

Zeke's face lit up. "They would either put it in a fuel cart or maybe one of the other planes." He realized there was likely enough fuel in the hanger to fill the 421. Zeke began running from plane to plane opening fuel caps and peering into the wing tanks.

"There's enough fuel in the hanger to fill the tanks up two or three times," he announced with a grin that spread from one ear to the other. "Why didn't I think of that? I think you're going to earn your keep after all."

"Earn my keep?" she asked accusingly, Zeke's grin was infectious, and a smile spread across her face as well.

An hour and a half later, they had transferred over two hundred gallons of fuel into their new ride, one five-gallon bucket at a time.

As Zeke was completing his preflight, his cell phone rang. It hadn't rung in days and the sound startled him. He hadn't even looked at it for reception since he charged it two nights ago. "Hello?" he answered on the third ring.

"Where are you?" his older brother Connor asked without greeting.

"I'm in Syracuse, Kansas. It's nice to hear from you, too," he answered in response to his brother's terse greeting.

"I'm glad to hear you aren't slobbering all over yourself and chowing down on people. How's the trip coming?" Connor asked.

"It's been pretty good so far. I blew up a school first thing this morning and crashed an airplane an hour and a half ago. It was a shame. It was a really nice Lancair."

"Huh, it sounds like it didn't fly too well."

"No," Zeke disagreed. "It flew fantastic. We put it through some pretty decent aerobatics and it was rock solid. The only problems it had were related to landing."

"Hold on," Connor interrupted. "Did you say we? Are you bringing your groupies with you?"

"Just one. There were four of us in the group when we started," Zeke said, turning somber. "We were in a house that was overrun. Two good guys didn't make it out."

"I'm sorry to hear that. We've had a bunch of good people die out here, too." Connor ratcheted down his energetic rhetoric in response to the memory of his lost friends and acquaintances as well as the losses his brother had suffered. He doubted he would ever completely recover from the ache the deaths had burned into his heart.

"How's the continuation of your trip looking?"

"It's looking pretty good," Zeke answered. "We should be home in a little over four hours. We're in the process of requisitioning a Cessna 421 Charlie. I was just finishing the pre-flight when you called. It's all fueled up and ready for departure."

Connor paused a moment. "When you say requisitioning, do you mean stealing? I don't know how they view it in Kansas, but in California, aircraft theft is a serious offence. Am I going to have to lock you up when I see you?"

Zeke laughed. "Easy there, Big Brother. I never said I was stealing the plane. I said I was requisitioning it. In the unlikely event it's ever reported as stolen, I suppose you could try to arrest me. I'm pretty sure it falls under squatter's rights or something like that anyway."

Now it was Connor's turn to laugh. "Okay. I can see I'm going to have to launch a full investigation when you get here. I'll see where the chips fall after that. If I get a report that it's stolen, though, I'm gonna have to take action. I think plane theft is the modern day equivalent of horse theft. In Kansas that's a hanging offence. If you're real nice, I might consider not extraditing you,"

Connor paused as he reoriented himself in his chair, trying to take pressure off his sore back. After finding a more comfortable position, he continued. "Why don't you make a layover in Lost Hills before you go to Mom and Dad's?"

Zeke thought for a second and answered, "We aren't going to have enough fuel to get back to Mom and Dad's from there. Is there fuel at the airport?"

"How would I know?" Connor chided. "I assume there is. The power is still on so the pumps should work. If there isn't any fuel, there are lots of cars in town. Most of them don't have owners anymore. I'm sure we can arrange a ride for you. I'm staying at a farm south east of town. Before you land, circle the area a few times. Once we see you, it'll take about fifteen minutes to get to the airport so plan your landing accordingly. There may be infected roaming the airfield. We'll see you in a few hours."

"Talk to you then," Zeke said and hung up his phone.

"That was your brother?" Meagan asked.

Zeke could see the pain of loss returning to her face. The gleam that had sparkled in her eyes as they lightheartedly hauled buckets of fuel was gone. Now her eyes were filling with tears as the memory of her own family resurfaced.

Rather than answering her, he wrapped his arms around her reassuringly and held her tight for several minutes before speaking. "You're one of us now. I know you've never met my parents, but they will receive you like a member of the family."

"Thank you for everything you've done for me," she said. "Outside of my own family, I've never met anybody who has shown as much compassion and generosity to me as you have. You didn't have to take me under your wing the way you did. I know you took on a lot more risk by dragging me along with you. You could just as easily have left me back at Lester and Mildred's." She stretched up on her toes, kissed him lightly on his lips, and then nuzzled her head back into his shoulder.

The kiss blindsided Zeke. Earlier in the morning, he had pondered a possible relationship developing between himself and Meagan, but it had been something that might occur in the future, not today. As his mind raced, he realized the kiss had signified their relationship moving from friendship to something more. The more he thought about it, the more he realized he was in favor of the change.

Chapter 33

Zeke took Meagan's hand in his and they walked side by side to the plane's open door. He stopped and helped Meagan up the stairs with a new-found sense of protection. They settled into the cockpit, Meagan in the right seat.

Zeke fired up both engines and did a quick systems check. Backlash in the gears of the Continental engines clunked and rattled at low RPM. Satisfied with the system check, Zeke moved on. "Push the brakes and hold them down as hard as you can." Zeke instructed. "They're the silver extensions at the top of the rudder pedals. While you do that, I'm going to open the hanger door. I'll be right back."

Meagan watched with new interest as Zeke quickly moved to the far side of the hanger. She hadn't planned to kiss him. It was a spontaneous action that occurred without thought, more instinctual than anything, and the fact that it had happened left her as surprised as him. She hadn't considered their relationship moving beyond friendship until that moment, but as their lips pressed together, she discovered her feelings for him ran deeper than she had realized. She smiled as she thought about the evolution that had just occurred between them.

Zeke activated the electric motor that opened the massive door fronting the hanger. It *rattled* and *squeaked* as it began to rise toward the ceiling. Zeke sprinted back to the plane. He pulled up the stair, latched the lower half of the door, pulled the upper half down, and latched it, too. Settling into the left seat, he fastened his seat belt. The door had lifted several feet off the ground by this time, and from what he could see, the path was clear. But as the bottom of the door cleared four feet, Zeke could see several sets of shoes running back and forth in a frenzy on the other side of the lifting door. When it had opened five feet, infected began flooding into the hanger. A teenage girl, seeing Zeke in the window, ran toward him. As she approached, the girl ran headfirst into the propeller and crumpled to the floor.

Before the door had opened far enough to allow the tail to pass beneath it, seven more infected had been diced by the huge spinning props.

"Okay," Zeke said, "Let off the brakes. I've got it from here." Meagan relaxed her legs and the plane began to creep forward. As Zeke gently nudged the dual throttle levers forward, the plane rolled ahead until the wheels came to rest against the bodies in front of them. Zeke opened the throttles to three quarter power and the plane lurched over the obstructing bodies. The aircraft rolled clear of the growing horde, left the paved taxiway, and made a bee line across the grass median to runway three-six for a crosswind takeoff. As soon as the wheels hit the concrete threshold of the runway, he smoothly pushed the throttles all the way forward, releasing all 750 horses to do their job. The Cessna launched into the air, leaving the bad memory of Kansas sinking away behind them.

Part 5

Lost Hills, California
Monday Afternoon

Chapter 34

Connor had been on the front porch of the farmhouse when he made the call to Zeke. He ran inside to the kitchen where Katie was working on lunch. "Guess who I just talked to?" he asked, effectively hiding his excitement.

"Uh, Matt?" she guessed as she continued slicing carrots for the stew she was making.

"Nope, guess again."

"Connor, I'm busy. Why don't you just tell me so we don't have to play twenty questions?"

"I just got through to Zeke. He's going to be here in four hours," he said, unable to hide his enthusiasm any longer.

"You got through to Zeke?" She dropped her knife on the counter and wrapped her arms around him. "You've been trying to reach him for three days. I was sure he was dead." She wiped tears of joy and relief from her eyes. "Where is he?"

"He said he was about to take off from somewhere in Kansas."

"What's wrong, Mom?" Toby asked, seeing the tears in Katie's eyes as he walked into the kitchen.

"Nothing's wrong, Sweetie. Your Dad just talked to Uncle Zeke and he's going to be here in four hours."

Toby jumped up with both fists in the air over his head, "All right! Uncle Zeke's coming!" He ran out of the kitchen hooting and hollering. "Luke, Uncle Zeke's coming!" they heard him yell in excitement as he ran outside looking for his buddy.

Katie turned back to the stew. "Is he going to be staying here?"

"No," Connor answered. "He's going to Mom and Dad's. I convinced him to stop in Lost Hills on his way." He looked out the window into the large gravel lot in front of the house where Toby was enthusiastically sharing his news with Luke, Matt, and Zack who were on guard duty. "I wish he would stay," he declared, his voice full of misgiving. "It sounds like his mind is made up, though."

"Honey," she said gently. "Maybe it's time for us to leave, too. You've done everything you possibly could have done for this place and it hasn't been enough. From what you guys have told me, there's nobody to protect anymore. We have nothing left here." She stopped as she considered everything they had lost -- their friends, their home, and all of their possessions. "We would have a lot easier go of it if we moved to your parent's farm. They have plenty of land, and the climate is much better for agriculture than up here. We could thrive there. If we stay here, we'll fight to survive, especially through the winter."

Connor knew she was right. There was nothing left to keep them in Lost Hills. The few remaining people would have to band together to protect and secure themselves. His job had been to enforce laws, not provide security. The sheriff department was effectively disbanded. The past few days had already begun his mental transformation from upholder of the law to hunter, gatherer, and farmer. He had still been working as the protector of the community, but he realized it was out of altruism more than anything.

People had to take care of themselves, and he needed to transition to full-time protector of his own family.

"You may be right," Connor agreed. "Lost Hills has some good things to offer, but there are some definite downsides. If we list them side by side, I imagine the negatives will outweigh the positives. I'm going to talk to Matt. If we leave, I suspect they will leave, too."

Connor left Katie in the kitchen to finish lunch and walked outside. Toby was still talking excitedly to Matt and Zack about Zeke's imminent arrival.

It didn't take long for Toby's excitement to vent. Once it did, he ran off with Luke to play in the bunk house.

"So, your brother made it out of Atlanta. That's great," Matt said to Connor.

"Yeah, it is," Connor agreed. "Matt, listen. Katie and I have been talking about leaving Lost Hills. The winters here are too long and too cold. It will be a constant fight to stay alive. My parents have plenty of land and the climate is a lot more temperate. With Zeke being down there now, we have an even bigger draw. We haven't made a final decision yet, but I'm pretty sure we're going to do it. We want you, Eve, and Luke to come with us. There are a couple other ranches near theirs and I doubt the owners have survived. If they did, we'll build a house for you guys on my parents' land."

Matt let out a long breath. "So you guys are out of here. I didn't see that one coming. I guess it makes sense though. There isn't any need for me around here anymore, either. Without land to farm, we would be fish out of water if we stayed."

"I don't think you'll have a problem finding land to farm around here. I suspect there's going to be a lot available if you guys want to stay up here," Connor said, offering an alternative to leaving Lost Hills. "On the other hand, if you do want to leave, my folks are going to need help making their place work. Without fuel to run the equipment, everything is going to revert back a hundred years. Or if you prefer, you can stake your own claim on a place near my folks. It's up to you, but we would like to have you guys nearby."

Zack had started walking away, feeling like a third wheel in the conversation. Connor started to say something to him, but stopped. "There is one downside," Connor continued. "There are a several towns nearby. Problems with the infected will be a lot worse there than here. Talk it over with Eve."

"We'll discuss it tonight," Matt said softly, still shocked to hear that Connor and Katie were leaving and even more surprised at the offer to move with them. "When's the move?"

"Like I said, it's tentative right now, but if we leave, it'll be soon."

"Okay," Matt said, nodding his head. "Let me know when you come to a decision and we'll go from there. If you don't mind spelling me on the watch, I'm going to go mention this to Eve."

"No problem, I'm locked, loaded and ready to go," Connor said, patting the rifle hanging at his chest.

Matt walked toward the house, staring at the ground in deep thought. Connor took off at a fast walk, catching up to Zack, who was starting a perimeter check.

"Hold up, Zack," he yelled.

Zack stopped and waited for Connor. "What's up?" he asked as Connor caught up to him.

"I wanted to extend the same invitation to you that I gave to Matt. My family owns a couple hundred acres of prime farm land in the valley a few hours from here. I don't know where you're from, but if you're looking for a place to start over, we would like you to come with us. It doesn't have to be permanent. You can stay for as long or short as you like." He didn't know what else to say so he left it at that.

Zack looked at him for at least ten seconds before he spoke. "You don't even know me. Why would you make that offer?"

"That's not true. I may not have known you long, but I know you. I know you are loyal and hard-working, and you care about people. I've seen you put your life in danger to help strangers. Tuttle vouched for you, too. His opinion meant a lot. I can tell he was the kind of man who called things the way he saw them. He didn't sugar coat anything."

Connor stopped and rubbed his head, "This isn't an offer being made out of pity. We probably need you a lot more than you need us. Your medical skills are invaluable. You know how to fight and how to survive and that's worth even more. If you want to come with us, I think it will be mutually beneficial to everybody. Think it over."

"I don't have to, Connor. I talked to my mom this morning. She has the sickness that leads to the infection and Dad was killed by an infected last night. Without them, there are no pulls on me. To be completely honest, I'm not particularly fond of Lost Hills, so I'm not going to stay here. If you guys leave, I'll come with you," he said as he put his hand out.

Zack's dopey grin gave away his intentions to crush

Connor's hand when they shook. Connor closed his hand around Zack's fingers rather than his palm and squeezed with everything he had. With his fingers tightly encircled by Connor's hand, Zack couldn't get a grip and was at Connor's mercy. As hard as Connor squeezed, Zack refused to acknowledge any discomfort when they shook hands.

Connor released his grip with a grin, pleased that he had one-upped Zack. It didn't quite make up for Zack's manipulating him into receiving stitches without anesthetic, but it was close.

"I have one more question," Zack said, turning serious again. "What about Martinez?"

"I was planning on inviting him, too. I'm also going to extend the invitation to Frank and his parents as well. I doubt they'll want to leave their ranch, though."

Chapter 35

Three hours after his call with Zeke, Connor was chomping at the bit. His excitement to see his brother was translating into extreme restlessness.

Everyone sat around the table after a late lunch, enjoying the conversation. It was the first meal Martinez had joined them for; up to this point, food had been taken to him in his room. He seemed to be well on the road to recovery. This was the first day he had been talkative. His brooding silence had been as much a result of the loss of his friends as it was from his head injury.

As everyone sat talking, Connor stood up. "I'm sorry guys. I just can't take anymore sitting around. I'm going to take one of the Hummers to the airport and make sure there aren't any infected inside the fence."

Zack, who was sitting at the far end of the table, put his napkin on his plate and also stood up. "Thanks for grub, ladies. That stew hit the spot. As much as I'd love to sit and chew the fat all day, we've seen what happens when Connor is allowed to play by himself. I think I'll tag along with him and make sure he doesn't get into any more trouble."

Matt wiped his mouth with his napkin and set it on the table as he quickly chewed his last bite and stood beside Zack. "Frank, if you and Martinez don't mind keeping an eye on things here, I'm going to go with Connor and Zack, too."

"We'll hold down the fort while you're gone," Martinez said as he scooped another bowl full of stew from the pot on the table. "As hard as Katie and Eve worked on this food, somebody needs stay and make sure it doesn't go to waste," he added as he rubbed his belly with both hands.

"Not to take away from your culinary masterpiece, ladies, but he always said the same thing about MREs. Give him an excuse to take it easy and he will grab on with both hands," Zack said.

Without giving him so much as an acknowledging glance, Martinez made a shooing motion toward Zack, keeping his focus on his food.

They ended up taking both of the Hummers they had reacquired from Curtis and his lackeys. Matt and Zack led the way in the first Hummer and Connor followed behind.

Nothing had changed in town. People Connor had known for years slowly meandered between houses and in the streets, merely shells of the people they had once been. At the sight of the Hummers, the individual or group would run at the vehicles. Most were far enough away that the convoy had already passed by the time they reached the street. Those who were in the street threw themselves at the vehicles as they passed. Matt drove the lead vehicle and Zack manned the gun turret. Since the supply of .50 ammo was limited, he fired with his M4. Even on the move his aim was deadly, a testimony to the tens of thousands of rounds he had put downrange in training.

When they reached the airport, Matt motioned for Connor to take the lead. Connor pulled up to the gate keypad, opened his door, and ran back to the second

Hummer where Matt had exited the vehicle and was standing in the open, firing on the small but growing number of infected running down the street toward them.

"What's the combination to the gate?" Connor yelled above the gunfire.

"It's the airport radio frequency, 122.7," Matt yelled back.

Connor returned to the keypad, input the numbers, and the gate rattled as it wheeled back along its track, permitting them entrance into the fenced off airport grounds. Connor pulled in and moved his vehicle out of the road, opened his door, and hurried to cover the opening until the gate rolled shut after Matt drove through. With the gate closed, Connor and Matt held their fire. As infected approached the gate, Zack cut them down, one after another. His silenced rifle didn't broadcast their location like the sharp reports from the guns Connor and Matt shot. With the vehicles shut down and Matt and Connor no longer firing, the number of infected dwindled until there were no more in sight.

"Zack, if you want to watch the gate, we'll check the area around the FBO and hangers for anybody who may have gotten stuck within the confines of the fence," Matt suggested.

"Ten-four. I'll man the gate."

A quick walk around the airport facilities proved the premises to be abandoned. Thirty minutes later, a faint, distant droning punctured the silence as the three sat waiting. Connor sat up and squinted as he searched the horizon for the approaching aircraft.

"There it is," Matt pointed at a light dot in the sky. The thrum of the engine increased as the dot grew in size. The plane made several circles southeast of town and then headed toward the airport. High above the field, the Cessna started a tight, descending circle, and entered a downwind for the runway.

The landing gear dropped smoothly and the engines quieted as the power was pulled back in preparation for landing. The plane began another left turn. As the plane lined up with the runway and the wings leveled, red tracer flashes streaked skyward toward the plane from a small depression directly beneath the aircraft. Two seconds later, a rapid series of booms ripped through the afternoon as the sound of machine gun fire reached their ears.

The plane pitched nose down and began banking as the engines throttled up and the gear was sucked back into the belly. The plane hugged the terrain as it built up speed.

Zack sprang into action. "That's got to be the rest of Curtis's crew in the third Hummer!" he yelled as he jumped into the back of his Hummer and climbed into the turret. Matt jumped into the driver's seat and Connor scrambled in next to him. The gate opened as Matt pulled onto the pressure sensor in the asphalt. He gunned the engine and the heavy vehicle lethargically accelerated onto the highway toward where the tracer rounds were streaking skyward.

Connor bent down low to look out Matt's window for Zeke's plane. It was now several miles away and climbing like a homesick angel, turning back and forth in a serpentine pattern as red tracer's continued to dart around it like angry wasps.

The road curved in a gentle ninety degree turn. Half a mile ahead, the third Hummer was still spewing lead at the aircraft, now far out of range. The phosphorous coating on the tracer rounds burned out in midair, leaving the previously glowing bullets invisible. The gunner and driver were so focused on the plane that they were oblivious to the approaching threat.

At four hundred yards, Zack opened up with short bursts out of his own .50 mounted to the turret on top of the Hummer. His first round was short, but he quickly walked the successive bullets on target. Hot lead projectiles tore through the vehicle. The turret gunner slumped over and then slid back into the interior. Gas from a ruptured fuel line ignited in the engine compartment, and the vehicle was soon completely engulfed in flames. As fire spread to the fuel tank, an explosion lifted the back of the Hummer off the ground before it slammed back down with a thud that bent the rear wheels out awkwardly on a broken axel.

Connor hopped out of his seat to make sure there were no survivors. The heat was so oppressive he couldn't get within fifty feet of the fiery off road vehicle. Although the smoke from the Hummer obscured the sky, he could hear Zeke's plane droning away to the south.

Back in the vehicle, Connor prodded Matt to get them quickly to the airport. Two minutes later, Connor burst through the door into the converted house that served as the pilot's lounge. In the living area, he found a radio. Picking up the microphone, he called out, "Zeke, are you there?"

Through the static came his voice. "I'm here," his brother's reply returned from a speaker mounted to the wall. "That was quite a reception. Are you sure you really want to see me?"

"That's affirmative. The threat has been subdued. If you turn around, you should be clear to land."

"Okay, I'll see you in a few."

Ten minutes later, the white Cessna pulled to a stop next to the fuel island in front of the pilot lounge and cut the engines. The rear upper door half rose above the fuselage and the lower half slowly opened, its speed checked by a gas piston connecting the door to the fuselage. Zeke descended the steps, then stopped and turned back to the cabin. Meagan ducked as she passed through the hatch, and Zeke reached up and took her hand, helping her down the three steps.

"Hello, Connor," he said grinning as he put his arm around Meagan's waist as she stepped to the ground. "It looks like somebody popped you in both eyes."

Connor frowned as his brother reminded him of the raccoon eyes Curtis had given him, but his frown quickly dissipated as Zeke reached out and tightly embraced his older brother. "It's good to see you, Little Brother," Connor said, voicing a sentiment he had feared he wouldn't have the opportunity to express again. After they released each other, Connor turned, and looking at Meagan, said, "Who's your friend?" His voice changed pitch at the word friend, taking away any doubt that he understood the relationship extended beyond friendship.

Zeke smiled as he said, "This is Meagan. We worked together before the world fell apart." Meagan's smile beamed as she shook hands with Connor. "It's nice to meet you. Zeke's been talking about you nonstop since we started our trip. I'm really looking forward to meeting Katie, too."

"Well, you won't have to wait long. She's back at the farm," Connor said as he released her hand. After introducing Matt and Zack, Connor added, "Why don't we head back to the house? If Martinez didn't eat it all, there should be plenty of leftovers from lunch. I'm sure the two of you are hungry."

Zeke and Meagan nodded their heads approvingly at the offer of food. "Before we get going, I'd like to fill up the plane if the pumps work," Zeke said walking toward the gas island on the far side of the plane.

"Hold on a second," Zack said, digging into his pocket and pulling out his wallet. "If the pump works, this tank's on me."

"I couldn't let you do that," Zeke interrupted. "Filling the tanks is going to cost at least seven hundred bucks."

"Not a problem," Zack interjected with a smile. "My credit card company just raised my credit limit to ten thousand dollars. I want to try to max this thing out before the network quits working. The only place I know of that's left to use it is at the gas pumps. Seeing as I have no intention of paying it off, we'll call it a gift from the Visa Company to you," he said laughing as he quickly slid the card through the reader.

Chapter 36

As the two Hummers slowly rumbled down the long driveway, Toby and Luke came running out of the house toward the approaching convoy. Katie and Eve stepped out the front door and stopped short of the steps, waiting on the porch.

When Zeke's door opened and he stepped out of the Hummer, Katie left her post on the porch and ran down to meet him. With tears in her eyes, she wrapped her arms around his neck and whispered, "We didn't think we'd see you again."

As Katie loosened her embrace, her eye caught Meagan who was now hesitantly standing at Zeke's side. Katie released Zeke and took a step to the side, bringing her in front of Meagan. Looking Meagan over, Katie turned back to Zeke and said, "She looks like a keeper," and then she gave Meagan a welcoming hug. "We're glad to have you with us, Meagan. Come on inside. Eve and I and will get you fed and set up with a place to sleep."

After dinner that evening, the group sat around the dining room table, swapping stories about how they had managed to stay alive. The conversation slowly ebbed away into a tranquil silence. After thirty seconds had passed with nobody speaking, Connor finally broke the stillness. "I know I've hinted at this all day and you are all probably expecting it by now, but Katie and I made up our minds. We're leaving Lost Hills and moving to my parents' farm."

Frank nodded his head knowingly. He had been expecting the announcement, as had everybody else.

Merv was the first to speak. "We're going to miss you and your family. You've been good to the community. What's left of it will be worse off for your absence, but I understand why you're leaving."

Connor nodded in appreciation at the compliment and slowly looked around the table at everybody present. "The offer I made to each of you still stands. You're welcome to come with us."

Introspective silence returned. Matt and Eve looked at each other knowingly before Eve nodded her head slightly to Matt. "We'll come with you," Matt said softly, breaking through the silence that hovered over the room like a heavy fog. He looked over at Luke, who was soundly sleeping at his side. "It's the best thing for our family," he added as he ran his fingers through his boy's dirty hair.

"Anybody else?" Connor asked as he again passed his gaze around the table, seeing if anybody else would accept his offer. Nobody met his gaze, each staring at his empty plate on the table.

Frank was the first to speak. "My family has lived on this ranch for four generations now. I don't know how we'll defend it, but this is my home and I couldn't leave it."

Merv reached up and patted Frank on the shoulder with a smile. "We'll give 'em a fight to remember," he said with a grin as he visualized making a desperate stand by his son's side against overwhelming odds.

Martinez spoke next, "I don't have any family left to return to. I haven't been here long, but I really like the area. If I can find a place to call home, I'm going to stay."

Merv quickly spoke again. "I think you've found that place right here. Welcome home."

"Well," Connor said, standing up, "I guess that leaves everybody settled. I'm going to bed because tomorrow's going to be a busy day, and I still feel like somebody beat me half to death."

-The End of Infected: The Flight

Email the author at theinfectedbookseries@gmail.com.
Look for the Infected Series on Facebook to Like it and see the latest info on progress for the third book.

A Note From the Author

I have always enjoyed End of the World movies. When I decided to write a book, I didn't have to think about the topic; it was definitely going be End of The World genre. Like everybody else in the country, I was hooked on the *Walking Dead* around the time I started *Infected: The Fall*. My enjoyment of the *Walking Dead* inspired me to center my book in the world of zombies.

One of the things that I particularly enjoy about the *Walking Dead* is the suspense of not knowing who is going to live and who is going to die. Nobody is safe.

Death is a situation with which everyone can relate; none of us are immune to it. Sooner or later we will all die. The fact that death is largely an unknown lends to the fear it engenders.

My question is this: Is death really an unknown and if not, what happens when it occurs? It is a question that every religion attempts to answer. Whether it is Animism of tribal cultures, Hinduism, Islam or Christianity, each teaches of an afterlife. What does the afterlife entail and how do we get to it?

If there is more to come after death, these are important questions to answer correctly. Contrary to dogma that is incessantly spouted today, there is only one truth. Two contradictory ideas cannot both be correct. They may both be wrong, but they cannot both be true.

Over the next pages, I would like to share what I have found in regards to death and the afterlife. If you are interested, I would encourage you to bear with me and read further as I think you will find it interesting, even if you disagree. If not, thank you for reading my books, and I wish you the best.

I have spent significant time investigating the religions of the world. As you have more than likely deduced, I have reached a conclusion as to which is correct. I am not going to spend time laying out the problems I found with the beliefs I have discarded. I am simply going to present a brief case for what I believe to be the truth and why I have come to this conclusion.

At the risk of ruining the suspense, I have come to believe that the Bible (Don't give up on me yet.) is the word of God and holds the answers to the mysteries of life. In fact, it makes that claim for itself:

All Scripture is given by inspiration of God, and is profitable for doctrine, for reproof, for correction, for instruction in righteousness, that the man of God may be complete, thoroughly equipped for every good work. (I Timothy 3:16, 17)

There are many factors that have led me to place my faith in the authenticity of the Bible. I will briefly present a few.

In my mind, the most significant proof of the Bible is the prophesies it made that have been fulfilled, and there are hundreds of them. For the sake of brevity, I am only going to present one:

For dogs have surrounded Me; the congregation of the wicked has enclosed Me. They pierced My hands and My feet... They divide My garments among them, and for My clothing they cast lots. (Psalm 22:16,18)

This prediction of the Messiah's death was written around 1000 BC. It was recorded some 500 years before the first known practice of crucifixion and was fulfilled by Jesus' death, which was recorded in the New Testament in the Gospels of Matthew, Mark, Luke, and John. All four report Jesus' death by crucifixion, the barbaric punishment in which nails were hammered through an individual's hands and feet, affixing him to a wooden cross.

The Gospel of Mark records the soldiers casting lots for Jesus' clothing at his death as predicted over 1000 years before:

And when they crucified Him, they divided His garments, casting lots for them to determine what every man should take. (Mark 15:24)

Another evidence that the Bible is more than a mere collection of moral teachings is its historical accuracy. Archeology is constantly confirming the Bible. An example is the discovery of the Hittite empire. The Hittites are mentioned many times in the Bible. Until the 19th century, outside of the Bible, there was no evidence that such an empire had existed and many used this lack of evidence as proof the Bible was wrong. In the early 1900's the Hittite capital, Hattusa, was discovered in northern Turkey. Further evidence of the Hittite Empire was discovered in Egypt in the form of a treaty between Egypt and the Hittite empire.

The Bible provides many scientific insights beyond what was known at the time. This one, speaking of God, is from the book of Job:

He stretches out the north over empty space; He hangs the earth on nothing... He drew a circular horizon on the face of the waters, at the boundary of light and darkness. (Job 26:7, 10)

Even relatively modern cultures have had many beliefs regarding the nature of the earth. The book of Job was the first book of the Bible to be written. Even thousands of years ago, through God's revelation, it was understood that the earth is round and is suspended in space from nothing.

Over a period of more than 1500 years, some 40 people penned the words of God. If the Bible were a book written by men from such varying stations in life and different cultures, it would be full of contradictions. The fact that it does not contain contradictions gives credence to its claim that it is indeed penned by men who were writing under the direct inspiration of God Himself. There is no other explanation for its consistency.

While these brief evidences are far from exhaustive, I trust they are enough to make you at least consider the Bible's claims.

With that said, what does the Bible claim? The Bible deals with a broad range of topics, but the overarching theme of the Bible is the restoration of mankind's broken relationship with God.

The Bible enumerates God's many attributes, the most familiar of which is love. God is also described as holy, meaning He is devoid of sin. He is also just and therefore cannot allow evil to go unpunished. To some, God's justice may seem hard to reconcile in light of the evil in the world; however, the Apostle Peter describes God in the following way:

"... *is longsuffering toward us, not willing that any should perish, but that all should come to repentance."* (2 Peter 3:9)

Rather than administering immediate punishment for wrongdoing, God is patient, giving people time to turn from their evil and embrace him.

God created mankind to have a relationship with Him. The requirement for that relationship to continue, however, is that mankind must be holy and sinless as God is. It is obvious that humans are not holy or sinless. And it is our sin that has separated us from God.

But your iniquities have separated you from your God;
And your sins have hidden His face from you,
So that He will not hear. (Isaiah 59:2)

The Bible is the story of what God has done to redeem that relationship.

In American culture, sin is a loaded word that raises people's hackles. We don't want our actions to be criticized or have limits set on what we can do. In the ancient Greek language, the word in the Bible that is translated as *sin* is a term used in archery and has the connotation of "missing the mark." In archery, the mark is obviously the bull's eye. Hitting anywhere other than the bull's eye is falling short of the goal.

Regarding sin, "missing the mark" means not obeying God's rules. Throughout the Bible, God has laid out how we are to live. In the book of Romans, the Apostle Paul tells us that God has written His law on our hearts.

...who show the work of the law written in their hearts, their conscience also bearing witness, and between themselves their thoughts accusing or else excusing them) in the day when God will judge the secrets of men by Jesus Christ, according to my gospel. (Romans 2:15,16)

This doesn't mean that we intuitively know every aspect of how God wants us to live, but we have been given a basic knowledge of right and wrong. Our conscience directs us and accuses us when we violate that knowledge.

The Apostle Paul also writes in Romans:

"...all have sinned and fall short of the glory of God." (Romans 3:23)

Everybody is afflicted with the disease of sin and everybody and has fallen short of the standard that God has set and demands.

Also in Romans, the Apostle Paul writes:

"There is none righteous, no, not one; there is none who understands; there is none who seeks after God. They have all turned aside; they have together become unprofitable; there is none who does good, no, not one." (Romans 3:10-12)

The prophet Isaiah tells us:

But we are all like an unclean thing, and all our righteousnesses are like filthy rags; we all fade as a leaf, and our iniquities, like the wind, have taken us away. (Isaiah 64:6)

While modern philosophy maintains that we are basically good, the Bible tells us that, at our core, we are not. How do we distinguish which of these differing philosophies is correct? The obvious answer would be through honest self-examination; however, it isn't quite that simple.

The prophet Jeremiah wrote:

The heart is deceitful above all things, and desperately wicked; who can know it? (Jeremiah 17:9)

Because our heart, or our core, is deceitful and wicked, self examination is not necessarily going to be a fruitful endeavor. Our very nature is to not be honest.

That being said, if I carefully examine myself, I cannot honestly say that I am a good person. I strive to do good, but it is a struggle. There is a constant battle within myself between doing good and evil. If this battle exists, then there must be something other than good within me. If I were truly good, there would be no struggle.

When I do something that people say is good, it is never for purely altruistic reasons. There is always an underlying motivation that I will benefit from the good deed in one way or another, either in this life, or as a reward from God in heaven. God is all knowing and understands our thoughts and motivations. In the book of Psalms, King David wrote:

O LORD, You have searched me and known me. You know my sitting down and my rising up; You understand my thought afar off. (Psalm 139:1,2)

In Ecclesiastes, King Solomon wrote:

For God will bring every work into judgment, including every secret thing, whether good or evil. (Ecclesiastes 12:14)

God doesn't just judge our actions; He judges our thoughts and motivations. Seemingly good works performed with selfish motivations become sinful before God.

Further evidence that mankind is not good can be seen by turning on the television. The news is full of reports of all kinds of evil taking place in the world. In America, we receive daily reports of murder, rape, robbery, and corruption. Around the world, we hear of terrorism, wars, genocide and the like. These are not the reports one would expect to hear from "good" people. These are the reports of people who are ruled by sinful desires.

Beginning in Genesis, the first book of the Bible, we see the results of sin. When God created Adam and Eve, He set them in the midst of the Garden of Eden. They lived in paradise and had daily fellowship with God. As long as they obeyed the one rule He had given them, not to eat from the tree of the knowledge of good and evil, they would continue to dwell in this utopia God created for them. However, with the rule, a warning was given: if they disobeyed, death would follow.

Eventually, Adam and Eve disobeyed God and partook in the forbidden fruit. With this first sin came consequences. They were cast out of the Garden of Eden; their relationship with God was fractured, and the work associated with survival became laborious as a curse was placed on the creation:

> *To the woman He said: "I will greatly multiply your sorrow and your conception; In pain you shall bring forth children; Your desire shall be for your husband, And he shall rule over you."*
>
> *Then to Adam He said, "Because you have heeded the voice of your wife, and have eaten from the tree of which I commanded you, saying, 'You shall not eat of it': "Cursed is the ground for your sake; In toil you shall eat of it all the days of your life. Both thorns and thistles it shall bring forth for you, and you shall eat the herb of the field. In the sweat of your face you shall eat bread till you return to the ground, for out of it you were taken; for dust you are, and to dust you shall return."* (Genesis 3:16-19)

Along with the curse on creation came the real punishment for sin: death.

> *For the wages of sin is death, but the gift of God is eternal life in Christ Jesus our Lord.* (Romans 6:23)

This verse has bad news and good news. In order to fully appreciate the good news, we need to first understand the bad news, so we will start there.

Sinning is like working at a job. A person earns wages for it, and according to the Bible, the wage for sin is death. Unlike the job a person goes to every day to earn a living, with sin he is awarded his full wages upon the completion of his first sinful act.

We think of death as the end of our life. In the Bible, death is a bit more complex than that and is three faceted. It does include physical death, but it also includes spiritual death, or broken fellowship with God.

Prior to Adam and Eve disobeying God, they enjoyed being in the presence of God. He would take on physical form and come into their presence and commune with them.

And they heard the sound of the LORD God walking in the garden in the cool of the day… (Genesis 3:8)

After they sinned, this fellowship was broken. God is holy, or sinless, and His nature will not allow sin in His presence.

The third aspect of the death a person earns as a wage for sin is eternal death, or eternal punishment in hell.

But the cowardly, unbelieving, abominable, murderers, sexually immoral, sorcerers, idolaters, and all liars shall have their part in the lake which burns with fire and brimstone, which is the second death. (Revelation 21:8)

Someone may say God must be unloving to issue such a harsh judgment. When we look at the second half of Romans 6:23 and see the provision God has made we can see that God truly is loving.

The fact is, we don't understand how offensive our sin is to God. Nobody criticizes a judge for sending a vile criminal to prison for life, and few would argue with that person being put to death. On the contrary, when a person perceived to be guilty of a crime is allowed to go unpunished, the judge is said to be unjust. We insist that crime be punished in our society and God insists that sin be punished. He is the one who created the universe, He is the one who created mankind, and He is the one who makes the rules.

The good news is that God has not left us to wallow in the mire of a hopeless situation that ends in eternal damnation. He has provided a means to escape the just judgment we have earned as the wages for our sin.

In stark contrast to the grim future we face, God offers the gift of forgiveness for our transgressions against Him. This does not mean our sins go unpunished. Leaving sin unpunished would be contrary to God's justice. His very nature demands that sin must be punished.

In order to satisfy His nature of justice, and at the same time satisfy His nature of love, God offered the ultimate sacrifice. Leaving His throne in heaven, God took on human form and was born a baby. This baby, Jesus, was different from the rest of humanity in that he led a sinless life.

For the first time in human history, a completely righteous person walked the face of the earth. Unlike the rest of world, He was free from the penalty of judgment. His freedom from sin enabled Jesus to do something nobody else could have done. He willingly offered himself as payment for the sin debt of the world. He allowed himself to be killed in order to satisfy the judgment of death that had been decreed upon all men for their sin.

But God demonstrates His own love toward us, in that while we were still sinners, Christ died for us. (Romans 5:8)

The amazing thing about Jesus dying in our place is that sinners are the enemy of God as evidenced in the passage from which the previous excerpt was taken:

For if when we were enemies we were reconciled to God through the death of His Son, much more, having been reconciled, we shall be saved by His life. (Romans 5:10)

This is a demonstration of the purest love that exists. Short of my family, there is nobody I would willingly trade for their sentence of death, not even my closest friends. Yet, God did this for his enemies in order to reconcile the relationship with them.

Without getting into a long theological discourse, God exists as a triune being. In short, this means that there is one God but He exists as three distinct persons or parts. Although it may be an overly simplistic example, an egg is similar. It consists of three distinct parts: the shell, the white, and the yolk, yet it is still one egg. God exists as the Father, the Son and the Holy Spirit. Each is distinct from the others and each plays different roles, but they still exist as one Being, if such a word can be used to describe God.

This becomes important in light of a statement Jesus made while hanging on the cross:

And about the ninth hour Jesus cried out with a loud voice, saying, "Eli, Eli, lama sabachthani?" that is, "My God, My God, why have You forsaken Me?" (Matthew 27:46)

In paying for the sins of the world, Jesus took upon Himself every sin committed by every person who has lived and every person who will live as well as the consequence for that sin.

For He made Him who knew no sin to be sin for us, that we might become the righteousness of God in Him. (2 Corinthians 5:21)

In those hours Jesus was on the cross, God's wrath was poured out on Him, the same wrath that should have been poured out on me and on you and on everybody else that has sinned or will sin. For the first time in eternity, two parts of the triune God, the Father and the Holy Spirit, cut themselves off from the Son. Not only was Jesus, the Son, suffering an excruciating death for the sins of the world, He was forsaken and cut off from part of Himself.

Considering the lengths God went to in order to redeem sinners to Himself, I don't believe anyone can make a reasonable argument against God's loving nature.

In order to satisfy the penalty of death on sin that God's justice demanded, God sacrificed the Son in place of sinners. Jesus bore the penalty for our sin.

Who Himself bore our sins in His own body on the tree, that we, having died to sins, might live for righteousness—by whose stripes you were healed. (1 Peter 2:24)

God's provision for sin is available to every person in the world, but just like winning a raffle, holding the winning ticket isn't enough. The gift must be accepted.

For God so loved the world that He gave His only begotten Son, that whoever believes in Him should not perish but have everlasting life. (John 3:16)

The key is "whoever believes in Him." Faith is the means by which we accept the redemptive gift being offered to us.

But without faith it is impossible to please Him, for he who comes to God must believe that He is, and that He is a rewarder of those who diligently seek Him. (Hebrews 11:6)

The only way a person can have his sin debt forgiven is through faith. It is not something we can earn. Our best efforts do not produce anything that is pleasing to God. Even if we could perform a work that was truly good, it would be tainted in His sight by the stench of sin that permeates our lives. It isn't a matter of doing more good than bad. If it were possible for a person to only commit a single sin during his life, that one sin would make him guilty and bring him under the punishment of death. Forgiveness from our sin is an unmerited gift from God. There is nothing we can do to earn it.

For by grace you have been saved through faith, and that not of yourselves; it is the gift of God, not of works, lest anyone should boast. (Ephesians 2:8,9)

Not by works of righteousness which we have done, but according to His mercy He saved us, through the washing of regeneration and renewing of the Holy Spirit. (Titus 3:5)

The forgiveness of our sins goes much further than simply relieving a person of spending eternity in hell. Part of the curse associated with the original act of sin by Adam in the Garden of Eden was physical death. That does not go away with the forgiveness of sin; however, those who accept the "gift" receive "eternal life" as promised in the previously quoted scripture, John 3:16. The spirit of each person who believes will be resurrected upon physical death and that person will be given a new body and welcomed into heaven, where he will spend eternity. Before His death, Jesus said the following to His disciples:

Let not your heart be troubled; you believe in God, believe also in Me. In My Father's house are many mansions; if it were not so, I would have told you. I go to prepare a place for you. And if I go and prepare a place for you, I will come again and receive you to Myself; that where I am, there you may be also. (John 14:1-4)

The hope for the resurrection to eternal life in heaven for those who believe and have accepted God's gift is given credence by God resurrecting Jesus following His death on the cross.

Now this I say, brethren, that flesh and blood cannot inherit the kingdom of God; nor does corruption inherit incorruption. Behold, I tell you a mystery: We shall not all sleep, but we shall all be changed— in a moment, in the twinkling of

> *an eye, at the last trumpet. For the trumpet will sound, and the dead will be raised incorruptible, and we shall be changed. For this corruptible must put on incorruption, and this mortal must put on immortality. So when this corruptible has put on incorruption, and this mortal has put on immortality, then shall be brought to pass the saying that is written: "Death is swallowed up in victory."*
>
> *"O Death, where is your sting?*
> *O Hades, where is your victory?"*
>
> *The sting of death is sin, and the strength of sin is the law. But thanks be to God, who gives us the victory through our Lord Jesus Christ. (2 Corinthians 15:50-57)*

There are many religions in the world, and each claims a unique path to God. The question that many people ask is, "Can I come to God through any of those means?" The answer comes from Jesus himself:

> *Jesus said to him, "I am the way, the truth, and the life. No one comes to the Father except through Me." (John 14:6)*

Jesus also said the following:

> *But the hour is coming, and now is, when the true worshipers will worship the Father in spirit and truth; for the Father is seeking such to worship Him. God is Spirit, and those who worship Him must worship in spirit and truth. (John 4:23,24)*

Whether we like it or not, if we want to come to God, we have to come to Him according to His terms, according to the truth laid out in the Bible. He is the one we have transgressed against through our sins. He is the one who made the provision for the forgiveness of our sins; therefore, if we are to come to Him, it must by His rules and not ours.

While there are many religious books, the Bible stands alone in its inerrancy because the authors who penned its pages did so under the direct inspiration of God. They wrote the words He wanted to be written and He kept them from writing words He did not want to be included.

Knowing this first, that no prophecy of Scripture is of any private interpretation, for prophecy never came by the will of man, but holy men of God spoke as they were moved by the Holy Spirit. (1 Peter 1:20,21)

While the examples I gave earlier of proofs to the Bible's veracity were brief, there are many, many more. As stated earlier, I believe Biblical prophecy is the most compelling support for it being authentic, but archeology supports its historic claims. I also believe it speaks to the heart of the problems faced by humanity where other religious books fall short.

I will be the first to admit that professed followers of the Bible are not always its best advertisement. We, like the rest of humanity, live in a world tainted by sin. We struggle with sin just like everybody else.

We should begin to live a life more in tune with God's proclamations on how one ought to live, but it is a process that does not occur immediately. Sometimes the difference is not obvious, but over time, it should become more and more so.

God calls His believers to walk in obedience to His word, not to earn salvation and His approval, but out of a thankful heart for the redemption He has offered us through faith.

For we are His workmanship, created in Christ Jesus for good works, which God prepared beforehand that we should walk in them. (Ephesians 2:10)

I am not a preacher or a theologian, and this is only a brief introduction to what I wholeheartedly believe to be the most important message the world has been given. My prayer is that the passages I have shared from the Bible will resonate within you. If they do, pick up a Bible and read the Gospel of John, which is the story of Jesus' life. I would also highly recommend a book entitled *The Stranger on the Road to Emmaus* by John Cross. It provides a better summary and explanation of the Bible than any other book I have read. If the price is too steep, I will happily give you a copy of the Bible or *The Stranger on the Road to Emmaus*; these issues are that important to me.

Finally, please contact me personally. I would love to have a further discussion if you are interested. My email address is theinfectedbookseries@gmail.com. I answer every email I receive. Although I would like to consider myself a writer, I also have a "real job" so I don't always get to my email every day. Be patient. I will get back to you.

About the Author

Caleb Cleek lives in a small California town with his family. He enjoys hunting, shooting and spending time with his kids. He is currently working on the third installment of the Infected Series. Feedback left on Amazon.com is greatly appreciated. Caleb can be contacted by email at theinfectedbookseries@gmail.com. Look for The Infected Series on Facebook for the latest information.

Made in the USA
Lexington, KY
09 January 2019